I'm inside the killer's mind.

Grayson was held powerless in the mind of the killer. She watched as the killer crept up behind the frightened young security guard. The guard was standing in front of an open elevator shaft. He never heard the killer behind him.

Then he was falling. His terror was like an explosion of fireworks before Grayson's eyes.

Grayson felt a flash of the killer's twisted glee, and then abruptly the sick mind released her.

The vision vanished. Grayson found herself standing in the kitchen again, her heart pounding wildly.

Other Thrillers you will enjoy:

The Waitress
by Sinclair Smith

Dream Date
by Sinclair Smith

Let Me Tell You How I Died
by Sinclair Smith

The Boy Next Door
by Sinclair Smith

Amnesia
by Sinclair Smith

Krazy 4 U
by A. Bates

SECOND SIGHT

SINCLAIR SMITH

SCHOLASTIC INC.
New York Toronto London Auckland Sydney

The author wishes to thank Dr. David
Lieberman and the New York Eye and Ear
Infirmary for their invaluable assistance.

ISBN 0-590-60287-X

12 11 10 9 8 7 6 5 4 3 2 1   6 7 8 9/9 0 1/0

Printed in the U.S.A.   01

First Scholastic printing, April 1996

For Ken Dooley

Chapter 1

Without a flicker of warning, the light went out in a single silent snap.

What's happening? Grayson asked herself.

She had been sitting in a room blazing with sunshine. It could not have been snuffed out like an electric light. Nor was this the darkness caused by an eclipse of the sun. This was the darkness of night.

Where am I? she asked herself. The tiny bedroom where she had been sitting was gone, replaced by a huge, high-ceilinged room draped in shadows.

As her eyes adjusted to the darkness she could make out an exposed brick wall to her right. On it was mounted one of the largest mirrors she'd ever seen, with an ornate gilt frame.

Grayson turned slowly, letting her gaze travel throughout the room. Everything in it had the patina of luxury. Whoever lives here is probably a millionaire, she told herself.

There was an open glass door that led to a balcony. Grayson walked through the door and out into the night air. Beyond the balcony railing, the lights of the Brooklyn Bridge spanned the darkness above the East River.

She felt a tingle of fear at the back of her neck and whirled around. There was someone else here. *She knew it.* She knew it the same way that she knew they intended to harm her.

Her whole body tensed, alerted to the slightest movement, the faintest sound.

Something moved in the shadows.

No! Grayson screamed silently as her terror mounted. She fought to keep the fear from overwhelming her as her gaze darted from side to side, hunting for an escape.

She took a step backward.

Then another.

With heart-stopping swiftness, a figure shot out of the shadows. Before Grayson could tell whether it was male or female — or even human — she was blinded by the bright glint of metal as a light from the street below bounced off something sharp and shiny the figure thrust toward her. . . .

A white-hot surge of terror flooded her entire being, and Grayson stepped backward once more. Then the world tilted crazily. She looked up and was astonished to see the trees above her head. They were flying farther and farther away. I'm falling, the thought flashed through her brain.

For an instant there was a white-hot explosion of pain that blotted out everything.

Then there was nothing.

Nothing.

Chapter 2

Grayson opened her eyes and saw the familiar walls of her room. They were papered with what was supposed to be a pattern of violets. Grayson thought they looked like rows of grinning purple gargoyle faces.

Although she was sitting firmly in a chair in front of her dressing table, she still had the sensation of falling through space. She was afraid she was going to be sick.

She blinked and looked down at her hands. They gripped the edge of the dressing table so tightly that it hurt her fingers to let go.

Grayson looked into the mirror over the table. Her eyes were wide, the pupils black pools. Her face was drained of color and taut with fear.

It was the second time since her last eye operation that she'd had the same frightening vision. The operation, a cornea transplant, had restored the vision in her right eye. Six months ago, she'd had the first transplant on her left eye. Before that, she had been blind.

But soon after the operation last week, she had begun to see things that weren't there . . . terrifying things.

I was falling. Grayson recalled the dizzy, spinning way the sky had whirled in front of her eyes, and the sight of the leaves on the trees so close — then suddenly so far away.

What was the shiny metal thing? she asked herself, hating the answer that lodged in her mind.

A knife.

That was why I was afraid and kept backing away. That was why I fell off the balcony.

Grayson shuddered. The blankness that I saw when everything disappeared was *death,* she thought.

She realized she'd been grinding her teeth, and stopped. Nothing *really* happened at all, she reminded herself. I was right here all the time. Right here in my room.

"Earth to Grayson."

"Oh!" Grayson gave a startled cry and jumped to her feet. Her sister Kara was standing in the doorway. Her dark hair was held back from her face by a wide velvet band, and she wore a fashionable brown suit with a short tapered skirt and matching pumps.

"Why are you dressed like that? Don't tell me you're going into the office on the weekend again!"

Kara nodded quickly. "I'm afraid so. I have to help get ready for an important presentation on Monday."

Kara had a job as an assistant account executive for Steel, Inc., a big advertising agency in Manhattan. She put in long hours, and often went in on the weekends. Sometimes it seemed that all Kara thought about was her job.

"I was trying to get your attention for nearly five minutes, Grayson. You looked like you were in some kind of trance. Something's bothering you, isn't it?"

Grayson looked at her sister's furrowed brow and knew she was concerned. But she didn't want to talk about the eerie thing that had just happened.

"I was just off in another world, daydreaming. That's all."

Kara looked at her for a moment longer, and then shrugged. "Okay. Listen, it's time for your checkup with Dr. Leeds."

Grayson glanced at the clock. "Wow, I didn't realize it was so late. Are you going to drop me off on the way to the office?"

Kara shifted from one foot to the other. "My boss offered to give me a ride to the agency," she said. "I thought it would be a good opportunity to talk to her about the presentation. But don't worry. . . . A neighbor can drive you. Her name is Mina."

"Kara! How could you ask a stranger to drive me to the hospital? No. I'll go by myself."

Kara frowned. "Nope," she said, briskly. "That's not a good idea. You'd have to take the subway. I think we should make sure your sight is good enough before you go running into the city on your own."

Grayson was silent for a minute. She knew her sister was right. She still had some problems judging depth, and the vision in her right eye was blurry. She had to be careful going down stairs, even stepping off the curb.

"All right, all right. But I don't think you should have arranged this without telling me. Mina will probably ask all kinds of questions about what it's like to be blind and about my operations. She'll treat me like some kind of freak, the way Aunt Elsie's friend did."

Kara groaned. "Oh, please, Grayson. She's nothing like that weird friend of Aunt Elsie's. Besides, if you're going to be staying with me in Brooklyn, you ought to get to know some people here. Relax, you'll like Mina. She's your age, too. So hurry up and get ready." Kara glanced at her watch as she turned and walked away.

Grayson pressed her lips together. Relax, she echoed silently. Easy for you to say if you're not the one people think is some sort of curiosity — the girl who used to be blind.

"Will you be seeing with some dead person's eyes?" a friend of her Aunt Elsie's had asked shortly before her first operation. Grayson had explained that they didn't stick someone else's eyeball into your head, and that the cornea was just the transparent covering over the eye. The woman had looked at her warily. "It still sounds like seeing with dead people's eyes to me," she said after a moment and stalked away.

Stung by her remark, Grayson had promised herself that she wouldn't give anyone the chance to embarrass her like that again.

In the mirror over the dressing table Grayson stared into her own blue eyes. What if what Aunt Elsie's friend had said was coming true? She had a creeping feeling of dread that it was.

I'm seeing the last thing the donor saw before dying, she thought. I'm witnessing a murder, through the victim's eyes.

Chapter 3

"Grayson, come on!" Kara called.

I'm as ready as I'll ever be, Grayson said to herself. She grabbed her bag and walked into the living room.

"Hi, I'm Mina." A girl in a pale pink halter top and cutoff denim shorts got up off the couch and extended her hand. She flashed Grayson a wide smile.

Grayson eyed the girl's hand. Meeting it with her own required judging the distance carefully. It wasn't an easy task with clear vision in only one eye. She smiled a little when she completed the handshake successfully. "Nice to meet you, Mina."

Grayson thought she'd never seen such long, straight black hair. Her own blonde hair curled wildly all over her head.

A horn beeped outside. "I'll bet that's my boss," Kara said, glancing out the window. She gathered up her things quickly. "I'll see you later," she called over her shoulder as she walked out the door. "Take care."

"I guess we'd better get going, too," Grayson said to Mina. "Thanks again for the ride."

"No problem."

As soon as the two girls stepped outside, they were enveloped in a thick blanket of heat. The street shimmered hazily in the summer sun. The leaves on the trees looked wilted. Even the brownstone houses seemed to droop.

"At least my car is air-conditioned, though I can't say much else for it except that it runs," Mina said as she led the way to the car. "It's my sister's old car," she said, unlocking the doors. "Hop in."

Inside, the car was stifling hot at first, but it cooled off quickly once they got started. "Your sister said you moved to Brooklyn to be closer to your doctor," Mina remarked.

Grayson swallowed. "Yes. Going back and forth from Pleasantville to New York City took up so much time. Now we're near the hospital, and my doctor has an office in Park Slope, too."

"You're going to like Brooklyn," Mina said. "Park Slope is one of the prettiest neighborhoods." She turned onto Flatbush Avenue, a wide street jammed with cars. "Kara told me what was the matter with your eyes, but I forgot the name of it," she said.

Grayson felt her insides knotting up. "It's called keratoconus. It's a disease that causes progressive damage to the cornea and can result in blindness," she said as if she were reciting from a textbook.

Mina glanced at Grayson out of the corner of her eye. "I'm sorry I'm so nosy," she said. "I just can't keep myself from asking questions." She tapped her painted nails on the steering wheel. "You must be so excited about sharing an apartment with your sister."

"It's fun so far." Grayson was glad Mina had changed the subject.

"My sister would *never* let me move in with her."

"Why? Don't you and your sister get along?"

Mina sighed. "It's not that, exactly. We're just different. My sister's okay, I guess."

Grayson soon realized that Mina liked to talk. She chattered on brightly as they drove. By the time they were in the middle of the Brooklyn Bridge, she felt completely at ease with her.

"It's too bad that it's too hot right now to go to the beach," Mina said, glancing in the rearview mirror. "It's the hottest summer ever. Some of my friends spend weekends at Fire Island or the Hamptons, where the beaches are a little cooler."

Grayson stared out the window at the Manhattan skyline. "I miss my friends back in Pleasantville," she said. "We talk on the phone, but it's not the same as being together."

Mina leaned down and switched on the radio. The steady beat of rock music filled the car. "You know what? I can introduce you to a lot of great people. I know more than a couple of cute guys, too." She winked.

"Speaking of cute guys," said Grayson, "there's one I've noticed in the neighborhood."

"You have? Well, tell me about him. If he's from the neighborhood, I might know him."

Grayson sat up straighter. "I see him pass by sometimes when I'm sitting out on the stoop. He usually carries a toolbox. He's tall and wears his hair back in a ponytail — and he usually wears jeans and a T-shirt with the sleeves ripped off." She smiled. "It shows off his arms."

Mina was nodding. "You've noticed a lot about him," she said with a teasing note in her voice. "It sounds like he could be Jared Moore. He works in construction every summer. I guess that's where he gets those muscles."

"Oh, you've noticed him, too?" Grayson laughed.

"Just a little. I've got a boyfriend, though," Mina said with a mischievous smile. "Listen, I've been planning on having a barbecue. You can come and meet my friends from the neighborhood, including Jared Moore."

"That would be great. Hey — we're here already." Grayson pointed to the green front of Manhattan Eye and Ear Hospital, which was coming up on the right.

Mina pulled up in front of the hospital. "I'll come back to pick you up in about forty-five minutes, okay?"

"That's perfect. See you." Grayson got out of the car.

Mina is really nice, she thought as she watched her drive away. *Maybe Kara's right. It's silly to worry about people treating me like a curiosity.* As she started up the walkway to the hospital entrance, her mood was light and happy.

But as she stepped into the hospital corridor, a cloud settled over her once again. In the midst of Mina's bright chatter, she had forgotten about her visions for a few moments. Now she'd have to tell Dr. Leeds about them. What would he say?

Chapter 4

"That's it, the examination is over." Dr. Leeds pushed back his stool. The wheels squeaked as it rolled across the tile floor.

Is everything all right? Grayson wondered. She searched the doctor's face for a hint of what he was thinking.

She might as well have been trying to read the surface of a mirror. The only thing she saw reflected in the icy pools of the doctor's eyes were two shiny silhouettes of herself.

A wide smile spread across his face. "Your progress is excellent. Your sight is continuing to improve in your left eye, and there is every indication that the operation on your right eye has been a success." That said, the smile vanished without a trace.

The doctor took off his disposable gloves and dropped them into a covered wastebasket. With quick, efficient strides, he moved to the sink in the corner of the examining room. It struck Grayson that Dr. Leeds was as precise and analytical as the machines he worked with — huge contraptions full of dials and numbers.

Perhaps that's what makes him such a great doctor, she thought to herself. He had the exactness of a machine. Emotions didn't interfere with his concentration.

Dr. Leeds bent over the sink and began washing his hands. He turned to Grayson and asked, "Any problems?"

"Well . . ." She hesitated. She wished Dr. Leeds would smile again. When he smiled, his face lit up with warmth.

Dr. Leeds stared back at her as he dried his hands on a paper towel. "If something is wrong, you've got to tell me. Whatever it is, I have to know," he said with finality. He sat down on the stool and wheeled it in front of her.

Grayson twisted her hands in her lap. "A couple of times since the operation, I've felt like I was falling."

"Do you mean you feel as if you're losing your balance?"

"No, not just that I'm losing my balance. I feel as if I'm falling off a building."

The doctor cleared his throat. "I think I'm going to have to do some further investigating.

Now, this feeling of falling — when does it happen? When you're standing or walking? Does it happen in the morning, or at night? Tell me as many details as possible."

"So far it's only happened twice. Both times were after the transplant on my right eye. Both times I was alone, sitting down. Once at night, and once in the afternoon. It happened today, in fact. Right before I came here."

The doctor looked thoughtful. "I've never heard of anything quite like this. First I'll have to discover if there was some problem with the donor. Perhaps he or she had some sort of balance disorder that's being transmitted. Someone else has the donor's other cornea. I'll want to see if the recipient has been experiencing any difficulty. Then we'll go from there."

Grayson sat up straighter. "Do you know who the donor is?"

"Not yet, but I'm going to find out."

"When you find out, will you tell me?"

Dr. Leeds shook his head. "I can't. It's illegal."

"But why?"

"Because it's classified information. It's part of the donor's private medical history."

"But I have to know!" Grayson blurted out, jumping to her feet.

Dr. Leeds raised an eyebrow. "Why do you feel you have to know?"

"So I can find out if the person was *murdered*," she said, sitting down.

"What in the world are you talking about?"

Grayson sighed. "I haven't told you the whole story. It's not just the feeling that I'm falling. There's more. I have visions. I'm in a dark room, and someone is hiding there in the shadows. They come toward me suddenly, and then I'm falling." She took a deep breath and continued. "It's kind of like looking at a movie with a lot of quick cuts — except that I'm in it."

She looked down into her lap. "The only reason I can imagine is that the last donor was murdered. I'm seeing the last thing that he saw — his own murder."

When Grayson looked up, she expected to see a look of shock, or even horror on Dr. Leeds's face. But Dr. Leeds looked back at her with the same flat expression he wore when he was examining her eyes.

Moments ticked by. Dr. Leeds simply sat there without saying a word. Grayson waited nervously for him to speak, hearing the muffled voices and footsteps from the hall, and the traffic noise outside. Dr. Leeds got up, walked across the room, and sat down at his desk.

"Well?" she said, when she couldn't stand the doctor's silence anymore. "What do you think?"

"I'm still thinking." Dr. Leeds drummed his fingers on the desk. "When it happened at night, isn't it possible that you were dreaming? And isn't it possible that you just dozed off this afternoon and didn't realize it?"

"No, no, no!" Grayson shook her head impatiently. "It *isn't* possible. I know the difference between what happened to me and a nightmare."

"Take it easy, Grayson." Dr. Leeds tilted his head to one side. Grayson could almost hear the neurons firing as he searched his mental computer files for possible explanations.

"Around the time we scheduled your second operation, there was a case in the news that got a lot of publicity. A man fell off the balcony of his Upper East Side apartment. The reason the case got so much publicity was that the man was very wealthy, and nobody could figure out how it happened. The police found no evidence of foul play, and the coroner ruled out drinking and drugs. So why did this man fall off a balcony? It was a truly bizarre accident, but those happen sometimes."

Dr. Leeds stroked his chin. "You might have

heard about it. It was Zeke Stuart. The television producer."

"Zeke Stuart," Grayson echoed. The name was familiar. She remembered seeing it in the credits at the end of some of her favorite television shows. Zeke Stuart had often been in the spotlight himself, as he frequented the trendy nightspots with his celebrity friends.

Dr. Leeds leaned forward. "What I'm thinking is that you heard about this case in the news at the time you were about to have your second operation. It must have stuck in your mind. There are a lot of emotional issues in your life right now."

"*Emotional issues!*" Grayson snapped. "I know what you mean by that! You think I'm imagining things. The next thing I know, you're going to be suggesting that I see a shrink."

Dr. Leeds remained unruffled by Grayson's outburst. "Well, with all of the changes you're going through, I don't think that talking things over with a counselor is such a bad idea. It might get you over some rough spots. You haven't been able to see for a long time. Your life has changed."

He crossed his arms. "Anyway, I'm still going to check to find if these feelings of falling are the result of problems with the donor."

As Grayson opened her mouth to speak, the doctor held up his hand for silence. "I've already told you, I'm *not* going to reveal the identity of the donor."

"But it's not fair!"

"Yes, it *is* fair," the doctor said with a tight-lipped expression. "Besides, it's unlikely that the donor was a murder victim. And if that *was* the case, it would be better for you not to know. How do you think you'd feel about it? Pretty eerie, I imagine."

He stood up. "I've got to get to a meeting. I'll see you next week."

Grayson knew that further arguing with the doctor would be futile. She got to her feet and made her way carefully down the busy corridor toward the elevator. As she rode to the ground floor, she wondered how she could persuade Dr. Leeds to tell her who the donor was. Then, as the doors slid open, it dawned on her that she didn't have to. What she really needed to know was not who the donor was, but how he died. She hoped Dr. Leeds would tell her that much.

Outside, she waited for Mina near a newsstand in front of the hospital. To pass the time, she studied the covers of newspapers and magazines.

A newspaper headline made her catch her breath. . . .

FOUL PLAY SUSPECTED IN DEATH OF MILLIONAIRE ZEKE STUART.

The article said that foul play had been suspected from the beginning, but the family had suppressed news of the investigation for fear of a scandal. Now the truth was out. The millionaire hadn't fallen off the balcony by accident. He had been pushed.

Chapter 5

That night every network carried the story about the mysterious murder of Zeke Stuart. Grayson's sister had left a message on the answering machine saying she was working late, so Grayson huddled alone in front of the television set. She watched news program after news program, not wanting to miss a single segment about the murder.

She hoped that they would show the inside of Zeke Stuart's apartment, or even the balcony from which he had been pushed to his death. She had to know if they looked like the apartment and balcony she had seen in her vision. But as the last program concluded, nothing had been shown on TV except an old picture of a very-much-alive Zeke Stuart flashing a million-dollar smile.

Grayson felt let down. She hardly knew any more about the murder than what she'd learned from reading the newspaper she'd bought that afternoon. But as disappointment settled over her, an announcer asked viewers to stay tuned for a special feature about Zeke Stuart's career and its tragic end. An eight-hundred number flashed on the screen for people to call with information about the murder.

As the sun faded into the sunset and the sunset gradually gave way to twilight, Grayson sat with her eyes glued to the set. Soon the apartment was bathed in darkness except for the glow from the television screen.

After talking about Zeke's childhood and showing the many highlights of his career and his glamorous lifestyle, the program turned to the subject of Stuart's murder.

The show's host announced that they would be broadcasting from the scene of the crime. Grayson's heart leaped. She watched in amazement as the program began to grant her wish. The camera began to move through Stuart's apartment while the host continued speaking.

"Because of Zeke Stuart's tremendous wealth, the possibility that the murderer was a relative who stood to gain control of the finances is a possibility that cannot be overlooked. But at this point investigators say that all family

members have been cleared of suspicion. They expect that by the end of the day tomorrow, they are certain that his business associates will also be cleared."

Grayson was afraid to blink for fear of missing some important detail. Painstakingly, she searched for furnishings that she had seen in her waking nightmare, but none appeared, as they went through room, after room, after room.

"As you can see, the apartment is magnificent. The millionaire had it redone to make room for some of his newest treasures. Yet the investigation hasn't discovered a single thing missing.

"One of the most expensive items is in the study, where a wall holds an imported gilt mirror worth an estimated three million dollars."

Grayson's heart lodged in her throat. There it was! It was the same mirror she had seen in her vision!

A chill passed through her body. How much more proof could I ask for? she asked herself. This must mean that what I believed is true — Zeke Stuart was the donor for my last operation. It's his murder I've been seeing.

She felt hollow inside. Knowing that the donor was murdered was indeed an eerie feeling. But knowing that she had viewed the murder again and again through the victim's eyes was even weirder.

The eight-hundred number floated across the screen again. Grayson dismissed the thought of calling with her information as soon as the idea occurred to her. Dr. Leeds's reaction was fresh in her mind. The investigators wouldn't pay the slightest attention to me, she thought. They'd just think I'm some weirdo.

The doorbell rang, loud and insistent. Startled, Grayson turned from the light of the television screen and drew her breath in sharply at the sight of the darkness in the room.

What time is it? she wondered, her eyes turning to the clock on the wall. Ten o'clock! I was so caught up in the news, I must have lost track of the time completely.

The bell rang again.

Grayson switched on the old brass lamp that stood next to the couch and padded toward the door. "Who is it?" she called, thinking it must be one of Kara's friends.

The only answer was another loud, insistent ring.

Grayson flipped open the peephole and stared out into the hallway. She looked as far as she could in either direction, up and down the hall. She couldn't see a soul.

Maybe someone had made a mistake and discovered they had rung the bell for the wrong apartment, she told herself. But she couldn't ignore an uneasy stirring in her stomach. Why hadn't she heard another door opening and closing, or footsteps retreating down the hall. Why was there only silence?

She turned away from the door, and the doorbell rang again, louder and longer than before. Grayson felt a twinge of uneasiness. She didn't like what was happening. In fact, part of her was plain, outright afraid.

I'm not going to let some stupid prankster scare me, she told herself.

"You show me who you are!" she said angrily, pulling open the peephole once more.

She looked right into another eye that was so close it was a mirror image of her own. The person on the other side had pressed against the door and whispered ever so softly, "I'm watching you."

Grayson jumped back and screamed.

Chapter 6

There was the sound of giggling and guffaws in the hallway. Even the thick carpet didn't muffle the sound of running feet.

Grayson's face flamed with anger and embarrassment as she realized she'd been the victim of a prank. Judging from the noise in the hallway, there was more than one prankster. She could hear them, still laughing as they stomped down the stairs.

She heard the outside door slam, and hurried to the window. Three boys, aged about eleven or twelve, trotted across the street, slapping each other on the back and laughing. She threw open the window and yelled into the street, "That was a stupid, childish trick!"

The boys didn't even turn around.

They were laughing so hard, they didn't even hear me, Grayson fumed, slamming the window shut. The super ought to fix the outside door lock, she thought. The pranksters were just kids, but if they could get in, then anyone at all could come right into the building.

Grayson threw herself down on the couch in front of the TV. The special on Zeke Stuart was finished, and the credits were rolling. It was only then that she realized that she hadn't eaten a thing since lunchtime, and she was famished.

In the kitchen, she investigated the contents of the refrigerator before deciding on cheese and crackers, followed by vanilla fudge ice cream.

She ate the cheese and crackers standing up in the kitchen. Then she fixed a triple-dip-size bowl of ice cream and carried it back to the television.

One of the fun things about living with my sister is that we're both crazy about ice cream, so there is always plenty around, she thought to herself, smiling. She flipped through the channels, not really watching anything, eating mouthful after mouthful. She had just finished the last bite when the doorbell rang again.

Grayson felt a prickle of annoyance. "Who is it?" she called without getting up. "Speak up, or I'll find out who you are and tell your parents."

A deep masculine voice replied, "Huh? Well,

all right. It's Jared Moore. You can tell my parents if you want."

Jared Moore! Grayson thought with surprise.

The boy went on speaking. "I wave to a girl who sits outside on the stoop sometimes, but I don't know her name. I haven't been able to stop to meet her, and I didn't want to wait any longer. I thought I'd stop by and introduce myself."

Grayson crept to the door and opened the peephole. It was *him*, all right. Her heart leaped with excitement. Now she wouldn't have to wait until Mina's party to meet him.

She started to open the door, then hesitated. Ten o'clock was kind of late to be dropping by to introduce yourself.

"I live right down the block," Jared said, "in number 603. Maybe you've seen me going into the house. You don't have to worry about letting me in. I'm not an ax murderer."

Kara said everything happens later in New York, Grayson thought. Maybe Jared doesn't think it's too late to stop by.

"You aren't saying anything," the voice came from the other side of the door. "If I came at a bad time, just let me know."

Grayson made up her mind. "Come in," she said, opening the door.

"Thanks." The boy flashed the same incredible smile that had made her heart beat faster when he passed by.

He's even more good-looking than I thought, Grayson said to herself as he stepped inside the apartment. He had the deepest brown eyes she had ever seen. He was wearing faded jeans that were worn and ripped at the knees, and a short-sleeved black T-shirt that hugged his muscular shoulders.

"I'm glad you stopped by. I'm Grayson Dean." She extended her hand.

"Thanks for letting me come in, Grayson. Like I said, I'm Jared Moore. I've been wanting to meet you." Jared took her hand.

A spark like a small surge of electricity passed through her body. In the brief moment that their hands touched, something happened to Grayson that had never happened before. By touching his hand, she felt that she had looked inside him and understood something about him. She had gotten to know him better without his saying a word.

Confused, she withdrew her hand. I'm getting carried away, she told herself. "Come on into the living room, Jared." She led the way. "Do you want a snack or something to drink?"

"Thanks, but no." Jared settled onto the

sofa. He looked at her. "You've just moved here, right?"

"I came here just a few weeks ago."

"So, what brings you to Brooklyn?"

Grayson could feel herself tense up. "I had an operation — *two* operations, actually, on my eyes. I'm staying with my sister so I'll be closer to the doctor. I have to go for checkups all the time."

"Really? What's the matter with your eyes?"

"Not much, now. I can see pretty well, and my sight is improving every day. But before the operations, I was blind." She watched Jared closely, trying to gauge his reaction. Would he treat her differently now — look at her as an interesting specimen?

"You have beautiful eyes," he said. "Such an unusual shade of blue. It's hard to believe there was ever anything wrong with them."

"It wasn't something you could see without special equipment," Grayson said tightly.

Jared was silent for a moment. Then he leaned forward, clasping his hands and resting his elbows on his knees. "I was born and raised right here in Brooklyn. How about you? Where are you from?"

The tension began to leave Grayson's body. "I come from a little town called Pleasantville, a few hours away. It's a lot different there, you know. Smaller. But still, everyone has a lot more space than they do here. Big yards — and most people live in houses, not apartments."

"There's never enough space here in New York," Jared said. "That's why I like to go to the park up the street. I go jogging there just about every day, rain or shine." He sat up and looked at Grayson with interest. "Say — do you jog?"

"You mean, go running? Oh, no." The whole idea of running made Grayson uncomfortable. "I'm just getting used to walking without a cane."

Jared shrugged. "Maybe we can take a walk through the park instead, then, and you can get in some more practice. The highest point in Brooklyn is there. It's called Monument Hill. Want to go sometime? Sometime soon?"

Before Grayson could answer, she heard the apartment door open. "Hi, Grayson, I'm home. What a day!" It was Kara's voice.

Lousy timing, Grayson thought. Kara appeared, holding a brown bag in her hand. "Look what I've got, Grayson," she began — and then stopped when she saw Jared. Her eyes widened in surprise. "You've got company!"

"Kara, this is Jared Moore. He lives down the street. He stopped by to say hello. We've just been talking." Grayson threw Kara a meaningful look. She hoped that Kara would get the hint and leave them alone. She didn't.

"That's great. Nice of you to stop by, Jared." Kara smiled brightly. "Anyway, as I was starting to say, I've got something special here." She pulled a container of ice cream out of the brown paper bag. "Chocolate almond fudge. How about it, Jared? Will you stay and have some?"

"You'll stay, won't you, Jared?" Grayson asked, turning to him. Jared was looking at his watch.

"I can't," he muttered. Grayson was surprised to see how distracted he looked. It was a startling contrast to the boy with whom she had felt so comfortable moments before. He almost seems like a different person, she thought.

"I really didn't know it was so late. I've got to go," Jared said shortly. He raced past Kara and opened the door.

Then he was gone.

Chapter 7

Grayson sat in the Brooklyn office that Dr. Leeds shared with his partner, Dr. Ganz, waiting for her appointment. In the short week since her last checkup, she had noticed an improvement in her sight. There were hardly any problems going down stairs or stepping off curbs. Walking over to the office from her apartment, she hadn't felt the least bit unsteady.

She knew the checkup would go well as far as her eyesight was concerned. What worried her was whether Dr. Leeds would give her any information that would help her make sense of the frightening visions that had appeared before her eyes.

She stared out the window at the trees and forced herself to think about something else. Thoughts of Jared Moore weren't hard to coax. What had made him act so strangely and leave so abruptly? In the days that had passed, she'd asked herself that question many times. She hadn't heard from Jared, and she hadn't even seen him pass by. She had spent more time than usual sitting outside just in case he did.

What about that feeling when I held his hand? she asked herself. It felt like I knew him somehow, and I could sense what a special person he is. Was it just my infatuation, and nothing more?

She sighed. She had talked to Mina about what had happened. Mina had told her that Jared often hung out with her boyfriend, Ron. "Ron said something about Jared being a little moody lately," she had said.

Grayson remembered the way Mina's eyes sparkled when she said, "Jared's coming to my barbecue. Maybe you can find out what's on his mind. Maybe you're just the person to cheer him up and get him back to being his old self."

She drummed her nails on the arm of the chair. "We'll see," she said to herself. "We'll see."

"You can come in now, Grayson." Dr. Leeds's voice cut her thoughts short. She picked up her purse and followed him into the office.

Grayson sat down and waited. She stared into Dr. Leeds's pale eyes and could read nothing there.

"I've checked into the condition of the person who received your donor's other cornea. He doesn't report any problems with balance or feelings of falling. No problems whatsoever, in fact. Certainly no visions of murder."

Dr. Leeds put his hand to his chin and looked at Grayson solemnly. "Have you given any more thought to seeing a counselor?"

"No," Grayson said firmly. She leaned forward. "Dr. Leeds, if you won't tell me the name of the donor, can you at least tell me the cause of death? That's what I really need to know. Maybe it would put my mind at rest."

Dr. Leeds surprised her by saying, "All right. I'll tell you that much. The cause of death was an automobile accident."

"Automobile accident," Grayson echoed. She felt as if someone had just knocked the wind out of her. Dr. Leeds went on with his examination. As he peered into her eyes, she sat in stunned silence.

At the conclusion of the examination, Dr. Leeds flashed Grayson one of his rare smiles. "Excellent progress. Remarkable, in fact. Now, I just want to say something about those visions of yours. . . ."

The door opened and a tall thin man in a white coat stuck his head in. Grayson recognized Dr. Ganz, whom she had met on a previous visit. "Excuse me, Jeff, I'd like to get your opinion on something. Could you come and take a quick look at a patient of mine?"

"Sure, Caleb." Dr. Leeds got to his feet. "I'll just be a minute, Grayson. Wait right here, please. I'd like to speak with you before you leave."

Grayson clasped her hands in her lap. She figured that Dr. Leeds was probably going to try to talk her into seeing some kind of counselor when he got back. She didn't care how hard he tried to convince her, she wasn't going. A counselor would surely think that she'd manufactured the visions out of her imagination, just as Dr. Leeds did. But I know better, she said to herself.

Then a thought occurred to her. What if the doctor hadn't told her the truth about the cause of death? What if the donor really had been *murdered,* but Dr. Leeds hadn't wanted to upset her?

He wouldn't lie to me, she told herself. But a fragment of doubt lingered.

The minutes ticked by, and Dr. Leeds did not return. Restlessly, Grayson got up and began pacing around the room.

When she tired of pacing, Grayson glanced at the clock. Dr. Leeds had been gone for nearly fifteen minutes. Had he completely forgotten she was waiting here?

Then her eyes rested on the stack of folders on Dr. Leeds's desk. Suddenly she was ablaze with excitement. Why hadn't she thought of checking the desk before?

Hurriedly, she shuffled through the folders. Harriman, Jaynor, Yi, and then — there was a file with her name on it!

Her hands trembled as she opened the folder. On top was a page of graphs and numbers that she couldn't understand. But behind it was a fax from a hospital in New Jersey. It concerned an organ donor listed only as ABT24M. The date of death was about five weeks before Grayson's operation, in the town of Montclair.

Grayson flipped hurriedly through the rest of the folder. There were a lot more charts she didn't understand. She had almost given up finding out the donor's name when her fingers rested on a torn scrap of paper. On it was scrawled in pen, *ABT24M — Aileen Mills.*

Aileen Mills, Grayson repeated to herself as she held the open file in her hand. What Dr. Leeds had said was true. The donor hadn't been murdered, after all! So, how do I explain these visions now? she asked herself.

Grayson was so caught up in her thoughts that she didn't hear anyone step softly behind her. She had no idea anyone was there until she heard the voice of someone so close that she could feel the breath on the back of her neck as she heard the angry words: "You've made a big mistake."

Chapter 8

You've made a big mistake. The words leaped out of nowhere and crackled through Grayson's being with the force of lightning.

She whirled around and faced Dr. Leeds. His eyes, which were usually so flat and devoid of emotion, blazed with anger. His complexion had gone a deep purplish red.

"You have no right to go searching through my files. They're my property." His voice shook with a rage that he was obviously controlling with great difficulty.

Grayson defiantly lifted her chin. "They might be *your* files, but they're *about* me. I have a right to know what's in them. I had to find out who the donor was."

The doctor stared at Grayson in silence for so long that the skin on the back of her neck began to prickle with fear. Then, suddenly, the reddish-purple flush faded before her eyes.

In seconds his face had regained its usual placid expression, except that his eyes were colder and paler than she had ever seen them before.

"I presume that you've discovered the name of the donor. I should never have left you alone here for so long, but what's done is done."

Dr. Leeds sat down at his desk and clasped his hands in front of him. "What I suggest you do is this. Since you won't take my advice and go to a counselor, I think you should try to put these visions out of your mind. If they aren't fed by your imagination, and you continue to adjust to being able to see, perhaps they won't reappear. As you can see, they have no basis in anything to do with the transplant donor."

He drummed his fingers on the desk. "I suppose you might as well go home now. Your next appointment is in two weeks."

The doctor began poring over some papers, as if he had completely forgotten she was there. Feeling dismissed, Grayson left after a few awkward moments.

She was relieved to be outside, to feel the bright sun on her face. What, indeed, would she do with the information she had found out? The donor wasn't a murder victim.

Grayson thought of Dr. Leeds's advice. What if she stopped trying to figure out the reason for the visions and just didn't think about them? What if they never returned? It would be a blessing, she thought. She told herself that she would just pretend the visions had never happened.

That evening there was unexpected relief from the oppressive heat. As the sun began going down, the temperature dropped, making the weather comfortable for the first time in days.

Grayson went through her closet trying to decide on an outfit to wear to the barbecue Mina was giving. She felt a mixture of excitement and apprehension. She wanted to meet people. She realized for the first time how lonely she'd been feeling with only her sister and her sister's friends to talk to. Oh, they were nice enough, but she needed friends of her own.

Grayson liked parties. It was fun to dance and laugh, and flirt with boys. She hadn't been to a party in a long time. The last party I went to was when I was blind, she thought. The thought kept repeating itself inside her head.

"Hey, it's six o'clock. You're going to be late," Kara said from the doorway.

Grayson sighed. "I can't decide what to wear."

"Somehow I had a feeling that was the problem," Kara said. "Let me think. . . . Are you sure you can't just go in a pair of cutoffs and a T-shirt?"

Grayson shook her head. "I'd rather wear something a little sexier."

"For a party in the backyard?" Kara rolled her eyes. "Okay. We'll find something just a little more glamorous than cutoffs. Follow me."

They went into Kara's room, where stacks of marketing reports were spread out on the desk and piled on chairs. Kara walked to a large antique wardrobe and opened it.

"I don't think you want anything too fussy. You need to be comfortable."

"Right," Grayson agreed, amazed that Kara had so many casual clothes. She hardly ever wore them. It seemed that she was always dressed for work.

"I think this is it," Kara said, holding up a short dress with wide straps and a gauzy layer of voile in a mixture of colors.

"It's beautiful," Grayson said, taking it from Kara's hands.

"I think it'll be perfect," Kara said. "It's loose and light, not too dressy, but a step up from cutoffs."

"It *is* perfect. Thanks a lot, Kara."

"I want you to have a great time," Kara said, smiling.

"I'm going to," Grayson said, firmly.

She *did* have a good time. From the moment she set foot in Mina's backyard, everyone made her feel welcome. In no time at all she was feeling like part of the crowd. I can't believe I was worried about meeting them, she thought, sipping her soda and looking around.

Then she saw Jared. He was wearing baggy summer trousers and a short-sleeved cotton knit shirt. As soon as he saw her, he walked straight toward her.

"Hi. Nice to see you," he said, giving her a little half-smile. He looked away. "You must think I'm some kind of jerk."

Grayson's mouth fell open. "Why?"

Jared shook his head. "The way I showed up at your house so late, and then I ran out all of a sudden."

"I didn't think you were a jerk. It seemed like something was bothering you."

"Well, you're right," Jared said. He frowned. "It's my brother. He's been running around with a crowd that's a bit too wild, and my mother worries. My dad's away on business a lot, and that makes it tougher." He stuffed his hands in his pockets and looked thoughtful.

"You know, that night when I went by to see you, my brother was the reason I left the way I did. I had my mind on meeting you, and I didn't realize it was as late as it was. I had to make sure my brother was home, or go find him." Jared shrugged. "As luck would have it, he was home, after all. I could have stayed longer at your place." He looked into her eyes. "I hope you'll give me a chance to make a better impression."

"Oh, I will," Grayson said, smiling.

"Great. I think that's enough about problems. Want to dance?"

"Sure." They joined the other dancers on the patio, and when that dance ended, they danced another, and another. . . . Then they stopped and talked for a while, and danced some more.

By the time they had stopped dancing again, Grayson was feeling that Jared Moore was the kind of guy she could get interested in. Very interested.

"I think I could use something to drink," Grayson said breathlessly, pushing her hair off her forehead. "I need to cool off after that dance."

"Me, too." They walked over to where there were coolers filled with sodas.

"Is there a seltzer?" Grayson asked.

Jared searched among the chunks of ice for a moment. "Here." He handed her a frosty bottle. She opened it eagerly, and began to drink.

"You know what I think?" Jared asked after taking several swallows of his own drink.

"What?"

"I think we should go out next week. What do you say?"

Grayson rolled the cold seltzer bottle in her hands. She'd been hoping Jared would ask her out. "Sounds good to me." She and Jared shared a long look into each other's eyes.

The mood was broken when a big red-faced guy slapped Jared on the back. "Hey, Jared, how's it going?"

Jared sighed. "It *was* going pretty well, Bobby." He nodded to Grayson. "Grayson, meet Bobby Grimes. Bobby, this is Grayson Dean."

Bobby looked at Grayson and grinned. "Hey, Jared, you sure know how to pick 'em," he said, slapping Jared on the back again.

Jared gave Grayson a look that told her he wanted Bobby to go away. Bobby didn't notice. He turned to Grayson.

"The J-man and I worked together on renovating Zeke Stuart's apartment. You know, the rich guy in the big murder case? Isn't that wild?"

"What?" Grayson was openmouthed. She looked from Bobby to Jared.

Jared's jaw tightened. "You know better than to bring that up, Bobby," he said. "You know that I don't like talking about it."

Bobby laughed. "Oh, come on, Jared. I think it's great that we were there. It makes me feel like a celebrity."

"You're a pain, Bobby," Jared snapped.

As Grayson listened to them argue, their words began sounding farther and farther away. A wave of panic swept over her as she realized what was going to happen. Then a haze clouded her vision, blotting out the light.

Chapter 9

Grayson held her breath as an inky void engulfed her. Her eyes closed.

When she opened them again, she was no longer at the party. This vision was different from the one she'd had before. In the scene before her eyes, she stood under a starry night sky. Grayson looked down and saw that she was standing on an asphalt road. She turned in a circle, taking in her surroundings.

There were large, shabby buildings on both sides of her. Beyond them it looked like more of the same, one after the other.

Starlight shimmered on the water just beyond the end of the road where she stood. A bridge loomed against the sky.

Grayson turned in a circle again, more slowly this time, trying to make sense of what kind of place she might be in. As her eyes adjusted to the darkness, she saw the loading dock next to the building to her right. Then she saw another loading dock, and another. There was one next to each of the buildings.

Warehouses, she said to herself. I'm in an alley between rows of warehouses. She tensed, waiting.

If only I could get out of here and back to reality before something happens, she wished. Then she looked up — and saw the body zooming down toward her from the night sky.

It was a man. He was large, and dressed in coveralls. For a moment it looked as if he was free-fall skydiving — except he wasn't wearing a parachute. Grayson caught a glimpse of his face, his features contorted with terror.

As the body landed at her feet she turned her head away, but not fast enough to avoid the sight. She thought that the image of the still, lifeless form would be forever engraved on her memory.

There was a flash from above, and Grayson looked up again. A dark figure stared down at her. Something in the figure's hand was reflecting the light from a street lamp. It looked like . . . it looked like . . .

Suddenly the image faded before her eyes. She heard voices, muffled at first but growing clearer.

"Somebody get some water — she's coming

around. Grayson, can you hear me? Are you all right?"

It was Mina's voice. Grayson tried to answer, but she couldn't speak.

A glass of water was held to her lips, and she drank. Then she opened her eyes.

Everyone at the party was crowded around her. They're all looking at me, Grayson realized with a flush of embarrassment. She wished that the ground would open and swallow her up.

"I'm fine," she said in a small voice. She realized she was sitting in a chair, and she tried to rise. Mina put a restraining hand on her shoulder and gently pushed her back.

"Not so fast, you. Take it easy for a minute. You just fainted, you know."

"I fainted?"

Mina nodded. "That's right. It must have been all that dancing. It's cooled off a little since this afternoon, but it's still pretty hot out here. Besides, I didn't see you eat a thing."

Everyone thinks I fainted, Grayson thought to herself with relief. The vision was her secret.

"Don't worry about it," Mina was saying. "It happened to me once when I went to Mexico. *Boom,* I went right out on the beach in front of about a hundred sunbathers. I was so embarrassed, I wanted to *die*."

Mina nodded toward Jared. "You should thank this knight in shining armor," she said. "As you were falling, he scooped you up in his arms and carried you over to this chair."

Grayson looked up at Jared. "Thanks."

Jared smiled down at her. "I guess this means I swept you off your feet — literally," he said teasingly.

Mina groaned. "Come on, Jared, that was so bad it *hurt*."

Grayson laughed. The crowd began drifting back to the party, leaving her alone with Jared. Suddenly she remembered what she had heard just before the vision overwhelmed her.

"Jared — I remember the night you came over to my house. I was watching the television broadcast about Zeke Stuart's murder. I didn't know you were involved."

Jared's eyebrows shot up. "*Involved?* Working on the man's apartment hardly makes me *involved in his murder*, for heaven's sake!"

"Okay, okay, I suppose 'involved' isn't exactly the right word. But you know what I mean."

Jared frowned. "The truth is, I'm tired of being associated with the whole thing. As soon as somebody finds out I was in Zeke Stuart's apartment, they want to talk about the murder. I'm sick of it. I wish Bobby had kept his mouth shut."

For a moment, Grayson thought Jared was walking away, but he only pulled a chair over next to hers and sat down.

"I suppose I understand what you mean," she said.

"Do you?"

"Yes, I do, I really do," Grayson replied. If only you knew how well, she thought.

Jared reached over and picked up her hand. "I'm glad."

His touch made Grayson feel a little light-headed. His hand was warm and strong. They sat quietly together for a while, looking up at the stars and listening to the music from Mina's CD player.

"It looks like the party is breaking up," Jared said after a while. "Would you like me to take you home? We could take a drive through Prospect Park and go by the lake, and I could show you Monument Hill."

"Just take me home, all right, Jared? I guess that fainting spell took a lot out of me."

"Oh, come on," Jared coaxed. "You'll love the park at night."

Grayson looked at him with twinkling eyes. "We haven't even been out on a date once, and you want to show me the park at night? Come on, Jared, I didn't think you were that kind of guy."

"What? Oh, I see what you mean. Look, I didn't mean I wanted to go parking. Really!"

"If you say so, but I'm still too tired to go for a drive."

"Okay. But we've got a date for next week, right?"

"Absolutely," Grayson said, thinking that nothing could be more perfect than a date with Jared Moore.

When Jared dropped her off later, he kissed her lightly on the lips. The kiss sent her floating upstairs on air.

But even the kiss could not blot out memories of her vision of murder. Grayson tossed and turned in bed.

Finally she drifted into a restless sleep. The vision, or dream, whatever it was, came to her again, replaying itself in slow motion. Afterward, she dreamed that she woke up in the yard at Mina's party. But this time the guests weren't murmuring thoughts of concern or inquiring whether she was all right. Instead they were chanting all at once, saying the same thing:

"It hasn't happened, but it will.

"It hasn't happened, but it will.

"It hasn't happened, but it will."

Chapter 10

The night's restless sleep left Grayson feeling tired and unrefreshed the next morning. Still, she was up and out of the house before seven o'clock. The promise of the day's heat was already in the air, but the temperature was still bearable as she headed toward Seventh Avenue.

The clerk at the newsstand looked at Grayson quizzically when she bought five newspapers. She carried the stack to a nearby coffee shop. There she scanned each one carefully, searching for news of a murder that resembled the one she had seen in her vision. She turned page after page as her eggs and coffee got cold. But an hour later, she put down the final newspaper without finding anything like the scene she had witnessed in her mind's eye.

Now what? she asked herself, twirling her

fork through the cold food. She looked out the window and saw two children laughing and jostling each other. She turned away and stared into her cup of cold coffee. After a moment, she decided that the only right thing to do was to go to the police. Getting them to believe me isn't going to be easy, she said to herself as she paid the check.

She was right.

"Let me get this straight," a detective named Lawson said, leaning back in his chair. His lip curled. "You say you have information relating to the Zeke Stuart murder. You weren't there, but you *saw* it. That is, you saw it *in your mind*."

The detective smiled, more to himself than at Grayson. "You say you saw *another* murder. *In your mind*, that is. This time you're way ahead of the police. We haven't even discovered this one yet. Doesn't that sound a little strange to you?" he looked pointedly at Grayson.

"You can make fun of me if you want to, Detective Lawson, but to continue to do so would be to ignore important evidence," Grayson said in her most adult voice. "I told you that I've been seeing things — having these visions — since my operation, and — "

"You said it right the first time," Detective Lawson interrupted with a chuckle. "You've been seeing things. Plus, it sounds like you can't be seeing things *too well*, since you told me you were blind just six months ago."

Grayson refused to let the man make her feel foolish. "I can see just fine now, Detective Lawson, though I'm not always impressed by what I see."

The detective snorted. "Look, young lady, I get stories like this all day long from people who are looking for attention. It doesn't make it any easier to do my job."

Disgusted, Grayson got up to leave. Then she sat down again. "Look, can't I talk to another detective?"

Detective Lawson sneered. "Well, I think you're in luck. Hey, Soames," he called to a man who was walking into the room, "this one's right up your alley. A real wacko."

The detective he called Soames was a bit on the stocky side, with a pair of glasses perched on a face that looked too young to go with the streaks of gray in his sandy hair. He sat down at the desk next to Lawson's.

"Go talk to Frank Soames," urged Detective Lawson. "He'll believe anything."

Detective Soames was unruffled. His eyes twinkled as he said, "Believing anything got me the greatest number of cases solved in this precinct. It works for me."

Lawson scowled as Detective Soames motioned for Grayson to sit down in the chair beside his desk. When she was seated he said, "Okay, tell me your story, as completely and as briefly as possible." He gave her an encouraging smile.

Detective Soames listened as Grayson described the operations that restored her sight. "Nothing unusual happened after the first operation except that I started seeing better. That's what's supposed to happen, of course. After the second one, though, I started having these visions . . . of murders."

The detective cocked his head to one side. "I don't understand. Why didn't you have both eyes operated on at the same time?"

"The doctor wanted to make sure that the first transplant was a success before doing the other eye. That way he could tell if he was likely to succeed or not."

Detective Soames nodded. "Go on."

"Well, the donor for the second operation was different than the first one. I got only one of the second donor's corneas. Someone else got the other one. My doctor checked and found that the person wasn't experiencing any of the . . . unusual side effects that I have."

"Such as?"

"It started with feeling like I was falling — someone had pushed me. I saw the whole thing as if I was the victim. My eye doctor thinks it's my imagination. The Zeke Stuart murder case happened right around the time of my operation, that's why. He thinks that these visions are some sort of fabrication I made up from stories I heard in the news."

"But you don't think so."

"No."

Grayson was sure that Detective Soames hadn't dismissed her as some kind of nut — yet. "Last night I saw another vision. This one was different from the first one. I looked up and saw someone fall. Then the person who pushed the victim looked down at me and held out something that glinted in the dark. The killer did that before, in my other visions. At first I thought it was a knife. Now I don't think so. I think it was a medallion of some kind."

Detective Soames sat up straighter in his chair. "A medallion? You could tell that, even though you were looking several stories above where you were standing?"

Grayson rubbed her palms together. "It's hard to explain, Detective Soames. It's not something I actually *saw*, but I *feel* that it's a medallion, rather than a knife. In fact, I think the medallion has a lion on the front."

A grin broke out on Detective Soames's face. He turned to the side. "Hey, Lawson, did you hear what she said? A medallion — with a lion on it, yet! That was what Stuart said just before he died. We never released that to the press."

Lawson gave a dismissive wave of his hand. "The information must have leaked somehow."

Detective Soames's boyish features hardened. "If I find out that anyone from here has been leaking information to their friends in the press, I'm going to make life so miserable for them, they'll wish they were never born."

Soames turned back to Grayson. "Are you sure you didn't get the information about that medallion from some other source?"

Grayson shook her head. "There's something else that may help. I found out the name of the donor and how she died." She shrugged. "Maybe if you feed the information into your computer, you'll come up with something."

Soames raised his eyebrows. "Quite a detective, yourself, hmm? How did you manage to find out who the donor was?"

Grayson looked the detective in the eye. "I looked in my file when the doctor was out of the office. I know I wasn't supposed to, but I had to know."

"Oh, well, now, that took some nerve, didn't it? Clue me in. Who was it?"

"Her name was Aileen Mills. She died about six weeks ago, in an automobile accident."

Grayson saw the detective's face turn ashen.

"What's the matter?"

"I knew an Aileen Mills who died in an auto accident at the time you describe. She was a psychic who worked with the police department."

Chapter 11

Barely fifteen minutes after Grayson had told Detective Soames her story, they were heading into the city over the Manhattan Bridge. Grayson looked down at the murky green of the East River. She had always come over the Brooklyn Bridge before. She thought that that bridge was a lot grander than this one, but the detective thought they'd have less traffic this way.

"You talked about seeing warehouses and the water in this latest vision of yours," he said, keeping his eyes on the road. "To me, that sounds like the West Side, around Canal Street. Lots of warehouses are there. We'll head over and see if anything rings a bell."

They turned off the bridge and were soon driving through a congested area where people hurried along crowded sidewalks clutching bags and bundles. Grayson couldn't help gawking out the window at all the store signs covered with symbols that looked like a cross between letters and pictures.

At a stoplight, she looked into a store window full of exotic-looking forms that looked like vegetables — but vegetables she'd never seen before. Two men carried a whole roast pig tied onto a pole.

"Look at that!" Grayson nudged the detective and pointed.

"They're probably taking it into a restaurant," he said, sounding disinterested. Grayson rolled down the window, which had a thin film of grime, to get a better look. She inhaled a fragrant aroma of spices. "This is fantastic! I didn't know this was here!"

The detective shrugged. "It's Chinatown," he said. "Could you close the window, please? You're letting all the air-conditioning out."

Reluctantly, Grayson did as he asked. She settled back against the seat. "Detective Soames, there's something that bothers me."

"Look, you've got to stop calling me 'Detective Soames.' It sounds too formal. Call me Frank."

"Okay — Frank. Zeke Stuart was pushed out the window of his Park Avenue apartment. There was no view of the water. But in my vision, there was."

Frank Soames thought for a moment. "Maybe the first vision was mixed with the second one, where you saw the water at the end of the alley."

Grayson shuddered. "So I was having visions of two murders at once?"

"I don't know, Grayson. Psychic visions can be like puzzles. They're not always easy to understand."

Grayson looked out the car window and saw that they were driving through a rather barren area with wide streets and large run-down buildings. They're like the ones I saw in my vision, she thought, tensing with expectation.

"My vision," she whispered. "It was nighttime, but I think the buildings looked like this."

"All right, let's have a look around." Detective Soames had no trouble finding a parking space. There were hardly any cars on the street. He switched off the engine and turned to Grayson. "You know what I've been thinking? Maybe the reason the person who received Aileen's other cornea didn't experience any of the things you did is because they had no psychic ability. Perhaps what happened to you is that after you received Aileen's cornea, you tapped into yours. You had the gift — at least some of it — all along."

"Well, I don't want it!" Grayson said in a

hushed voice. "It's awful having this thing happen out of the blue, and seeing these murders again and again."

The detective opened the door. "You may think so, but think about this: you could help us catch a killer." He stepped into the street. "Come on, let's see if being on foot helps you remember." He started walking. Grayson took a deep breath, got out of the car, and followed.

Over an hour later, after walking for what seemed like forever, nothing looked quite right. All of the buildings looked a little like the one she had seen; but even when she tried to picture them in darkness, she was sure that she hadn't found the one that matched exactly.

"Maybe we'd better try another place," Frank suggested. "Phew" — he shook his head — "I hoped we'd get lucky. Who knows — it could be anywhere — Brooklyn, Queens, the Bronx, even another state."

Grayson felt a mixture of disappointment and relief. "Maybe what I saw wasn't real," she said. "Maybe it was just part of some kind of riddle."

They were walking back to the car when she stopped suddenly. "Wait a minute. Why didn't I think of this sooner?"

"What?"

"I was standing in the alley *behind* the buildings. No wonder nothing looks right. We've got to go 'round the back."

"Let's do it, then," Detective Soames agreed.

No sooner had they turned into the alley at the end of the row of warehouses than Grayson's heart began to beat faster. "I'm not positive, but I think this is it."

She stood beside a loading dock and stared up at a padlocked iron gate. "This one," she said.

Beside the iron gate was a heavy wooden door. The detective gave it a push with his shoulder, but it didn't budge. "It must be locked from inside. Let's go around the front."

A shadow fell across the door. "I'm the watchman for this building. What do you folks want?" a voice behind them asked.

They turned around. "We're looking for someone who works here." Detective Soames flashed his badge.

For an awful moment, Grayson thought she would pass out.

"That's the man who fell from the building," she whispered to the detective. She put her hands over her eyes. "The last time I saw him, he was dead."

Chapter 12

Reality had been turned inside out. The watchman stood before Grayson, very much alive. In her mind's eye, she saw him lying on the ground, staring up at her with sightless, unblinking eyes, his body motionless. She turned her face away.

"What's going on here?" asked the middle-aged watchman, a clear edge of impatience in his voice. His eyes fixed Grayson with a narrow gaze of suspicion.

Haltingly, Grayson explained what she had seen. "Someone lured you up on the roof and pushed you off, right over there," she said, pointing. "It was a figure in black clothes, wearing a shiny medallion."

The watchman burst out laughing. It was a snorting, derisive sound. "Look, lady, you said you saw me being pushed over the edge of the warehouse. Yet here I am. You mumbo-jumbo people give me a headache," he said harshly.

Then he stopped talking and frowned. His voice softened. "Listen, I'm sure you're a very nice young lady." He turned to the detective. "Responsible adults shouldn't encourage young people to get these strange ideas," he said, glaring. "Now, if you don't mind, I'd like to get back to work." He trudged away without so much as a backward glance.

"We've got to stop him, Frank!" Grayson said. "He can't stay here." Her voice dropped to nearly a whisper. "If he doesn't get away, he'll be killed."

"Maybe not."

"What do you mean?"

The detective slouched against the building. "Like anyone else, sometimes psychics are just plain wrong."

"But what if I'm not? What if this watchman stands a chance of being murdered? Aren't you going to do anything?"

Frank shook his head. "Nope. I can't go around telling people they can't go to work because they're going to be murdered. Anyway, as you can see, the watchman didn't believe you."

Stung by the detective's callous attitude, Grayson turned her back on him. She stared out over the water.

"You're right," she said, turning back to the detective after a moment. "This whole thing was a mistake. I want to go home." She ran toward the car.

Later that night, Grayson got ready for her first date with Jared. She looked in the mirror and told herself for the hundredth time since that afternoon that she was not, *was not* psychic.

It's just as Dr. Leeds told me, she said to herself as she put on her lipstick, I imagined it all somehow — or I was dreaming. But I'm not going to do it anymore. I'm just a regular girl, not some psychic who has visions of murder. And I'm going to have a wonderful time tonight, with a wonderful guy.

Unfortunately, the date didn't start off very well. Jared walked her out to his car and then made a sad discovery. He'd locked his keys inside.

"I had my mind on you, and I wasn't paying attention," Jared said, giving his head a disgusted shake.

"I'm flattered, but it's too bad," Grayson replied, seeing her dreams of a wonderful evening beginning to vanish.

"Don't worry," Jared snapped his fingers.

"Just get me a coat hanger. We'll be out of here in a jiffy."

Grayson went back to the apartment and returned with the hanger. She watched Jared straighten the hanger out, and put a little bend at one end. He slipped the coat hanger in between the front and rear windows, and lifted the lock button with ease.

"Wow," she said. "You really did it."

"Surprised?" he asked, as he opened the door for her. He gave her a teasing grin as he slid behind the wheel. "I don't just break into cars — I can pick locks, too. I learned it from my aunt."

"Oh, come on, now. You're kidding."

Jared's eyes twinkled. "Well, my aunt really is a locksmith. Anyway, I've got another surprise for you."

"What's that?"

"*Where we're going* is the surprise."

"You're really not going to tell me?"

"I can't. Then it wouldn't be a surprise."

Soon they were zipping past houses and apartment buildings on Ocean Avenue.

"How about a hint?"

"Not a chance."

Grayson settled back into the seat. "Okay. I like surprises." She studied Jared's profile. "How's your brother?"

As she saw Jared's jaw tense, Grayson wished she hadn't asked the question.

"He's not much better."

"I'm sorry to hear that."

Jared touched her hand. "Never mind. It will get straightened out."

In another fifteen minutes they were pulling into a parking lot. Grayson saw a dizzying whirl of lights from a Ferris wheel, a roller coaster, and dozens of other bright, whirling rides. As they got out of the car she could already smell the cotton candy and feel a breeze from the ocean.

"What is this place?" she asked.

"Ever heard of Coney Island?"

"Sure. I've read about it, and my parents talked about it. I didn't think it was here anymore."

Jared took her arm, and they started walking toward the entrance. "This place was a big resort when my grandparents were young. It's a bit shabby now, but I think it's sort of funky."

Grayson looked around. The place had the feel of a tawdry carnival — only bigger.

"Here's what I've got planned," Jared said. "My two favorite rides here are the Cyclone — that's the roller coaster — and the Wonder Wheel. We go on the two rides, and then we head over to Nathan's for the best hot dogs you've ever had."

Grayson eyed the Cyclone. The cars zoomed to the top of the roller coaster, then went speeding down, dropping sharply as the passengers shrieked in delighted fear. "Eating after we go on the rides is a good idea. I don't think I'd want to have a hot dog *before* I got on that thing."

Moments later, the attendant was fastening them into their seats. And then the ride began its dizzying, twisting journey.

Up and down and around they went, forward, backward, and forward again, then down into a dizzying descent. Grayson nestled close into Jared's arms, glad for his strong embrace.

"My knees are wobbling," she laughed when they got off.

"Mine too." Jared laughed, taking her hand. They strolled to a cotton-candy counter and bought one of the fluffy pink clouds to share.

"What's wrong?" she asked, watching Jared massaging his shoulder absently.

He shrugged. "Nothing much. A piece of lumber hit me when I was at the job today." He shrugged. "I'll be all right. At least, working construction, I don't have to worry about putting in time at the gym."

"You're right, you don't," Grayson said,

smiling at him flirtatiously. Jared laughed, and then surprised her by blushing slightly. He's absolutely charming, she thought, looking at him.

They strolled along amid the noise and lights, sharing the cotton candy until it was gone. "Ready for the Wonder Wheel?" Jared asked, pointing to a huge Ferris wheel with an extra added attraction. The cars swung back and forth, out and back.

"Well, I survived the Cyclone. I guess I can survive this. Let's go."

Moments later, they were high above the ground.

"I think I spoke too soon. This is worse than the Cyclone." Grayson laughed. Jared put his arm around her shoulders.

The car paused near the top, and began to swing back and forth, out over the park. Grayson saw the lights and the dizzying swirl of activity below. Beyond the edge of Coney Island, she saw the dark expanse of the water.

A chill swept through her, until she felt cold all over. When she had looked out over the water near the warehouse that afternoon, something had started to bother her, but she hadn't known what it was. Now she did. *There had been no bridge, but there had been one in her vision. Why was the bridge missing this time?* She had a feeling that she wouldn't like the reason. She was still trying to figure out what it was when she felt Jared's hand on the back of her neck.

Chapter 13

Grayson turned her head sharply and shrieked. As if the scream triggered the control switch, the ride started up again with a jolt. Jared moved his hand from the back of her neck and gripped the safety bar.

"What's the matter?" he asked Grayson. "You're kind of jumpy, and your skin is cold. Are you scared?"

Grayson looked into his deep brown eyes. "No, I'm not scared. You just surprised me, that's all."

"Sorry." Jared leaned over and kissed her lightly on the lips. His mouth tasted faintly of cotton candy. The kiss lasted a long time.

The Wonder Wheel circled again, the cars swinging out over Coney Island. Then the ride was over. Grayson's legs felt rubbery as she climbed from the car.

"That was really fun," she told Jared over

hot dogs at Nathan's. Instead of standing up at one of the open-air counters overlooking Surf Avenue, they sat in the tiny old-fashioned dining room around the side of the restaurant. They were the only ones there.

Jared was right, she decided. These were the best hot dogs she'd ever had. But it wasn't just the hot dogs — *everything* was wonderful. Especially Jared. "I hope we're going to see a lot of each other," Jared said, looking into her eyes. "I still want to show you my favorite spot in the park. Then you'll be able to say you stood at the highest point in Brooklyn."

Grayson wiped mustard off her hand onto a napkin. "Monument Hill."

"You remembered."

How could I forget? she thought. He mentions the place every time I see him. Oh, well, it would probably be nice to go anywhere with Jared, including Monument Hill.

Jared glanced at his watch. "I've got to get going," he said abruptly. "I've got to check around some places for my brother and make sure he doesn't stay out all night long. He'll probably end up trying to pick a fight with me, and I've got to get up early in the morning for work. Sorry." He reached over and gave Grayson's hand a squeeze.

His touch was different than before. This time, Grayson felt a surge of anger radiating from him. She pulled her hand away, but Jared didn't seem to notice her alarm. He just got up and started for the door.

On the way home Jared was quiet. After a few futile attempts at conversation, Grayson gave up and stared out the window.

Her thoughts turned to the watchman. *I should have found a way to convince Frank to make him get away from there*, she thought, with a sense of foreboding that deepened as the ride went on.

"Here we are," Jared's voice cut into her thoughts. He pulled the car in front of the brownstone where she lived. "Good night," he said briefly.

After a moment of sitting in silence, Grayson got out of the car. "Good night," she murmured, her feelings jumbled in confusion.

"Wait," Jared called after her as she began walking away. Grayson turned around.

Grayson stood still for a moment. Then it was as if something took hold of her and propelled her into doing what she did next. She walked the few steps back to Jared's car and got in. Jared looked at her quizzically.

"Listen, Jared. I really like you. That's why

I'm going to tell you something . . . and I hope you'll be open-minded because it sounds, well, unusual."

Jared nodded slowly. "I'll try to be as open-minded as I can."

Grayson swallowed. "All right, here goes. You know that Zeke Stuart murder?"

"You seem awfully interested in it."

"Yes, well, there's a reason. It's because I saw the murder in a vision. Now, before you decide I'm bonkers, let me explain.

"Ever since I had my last cornea transplant, I've been having visions of murders. I found out that the donor was a psychic who worked with the police department on the case. Somehow, her psychic ability has been passed on to me."

Jared was staring at her intently. Does he think I'm insane? she wondered. Or maybe just goofy, like those people who go on TV talk shows and talk about being friends with aliens from outer space? Whatever he thought, she'd gone too far to turn back now.

"When I was getting ready for our date, I tried to tell myself that these visions were just my imagination. But I know it isn't true. I don't want to be mixed up in finding a killer, but I don't have a choice. I'm going to work with the police to solve the case."

"That's quite a story," Jared said. "It's pretty wild. I guess it's possible, though. I believe there are people who have psychic powers. Obviously, the police department does, if they use psychics to solve cases."

"That's not all I wanted to say." Grayson took a deep breath and plunged ahead. She kept her eyes averted from Jared's face. "We both have so much on our minds — you with your brother and me with this case — maybe we should wait a little before we go out again. Maybe it's not the best time for us to start seeing each other. We're both too distracted."

When she looked at Jared, she saw him staring at her with a cold, stony expression. "If you don't want to see me, fine. Look, I've really got to go."

"That's not what I meant at all, Jared," Grayson said hurriedly. "I just meant that there's so much going on now, maybe we should wait until things calm down a little." Jared looked straight ahead. "Never mind the speech. Like I said, I've got to go. I'll see you around."

Grayson let her hand linger on the door handle for a moment. When Jared didn't say anything else, she got out of the car. She barely had time to close the door when Jared stepped on the accelerator and sped away.

Wrapped in a dark cloud, Grayson trudged up the walk and opened the door. Dragging her feet, she went upstairs.

Inside, the apartment was dark and silent. "Kara?" she called. There was no answer. Of course it's much too early for Kara to get in, she thought as she turned on the light.

Grayson paced around the house restlessly. Finally she turned on the television set and flipped aimlessly from channel to channel.

She couldn't pay attention to any of the programs. After trying to watch for a few minutes, she put down the remote and let her mind wander. Thoughts of Jared and worries about what she had seen in her last vision mingled like wisps of smoke. Gradually, her eyelids grew heavy and she drifted off to sleep.

When she opened her eyes, the morning news was on. The sight of the face on the television screen jolted her awake in an instant. It was the watchman she had spoken with yesterday. He was being interviewed.

"I couldn't believe it happened," the watchman was saying. He was clearly enjoying all the attention.

"I worked a double shift last night. I had just made my rounds when I heard a noise coming from the roof. At first I thought I was just tired, and my mind was playing tricks on me. Then I heard the noise again, and this time I knew I'd heard it for sure. I thought maybe it was the building settling, or maybe some of the new construction had fallen in. They're converting the place into condominiums, you know." The watchman looked as if the fact made him feel proud.

The newscaster was holding the microphone close to the man's face. "Tell us what happened then."

The watchman beamed. "Well, I'm used to trouble, so I wasn't scared. I went up on the roof to investigate. All the while I was going up the stairs I kept hearing the tap-tap-tapping, like whoever was up there wanted me to know about it.

"When I got up to the roof, I started having a look around. It was quiet as can be. I didn't see a soul. Then I heard something over near the edge of the roof, so I went to investigate. That's when it happened."

"What?"

"Somebody came at me from out of the shadows, then ran toward me. They were holding something out at me, like they wanted me to look at it. It was something on a chain around their neck. A medallion, I think. I didn't get a good look at it because then I started to lose my balance, and for a minute I thought I was finished."

The newscaster faced the camera, solemnly addressing everyone out there in television land. "What this man is going to tell you next is so truly incredible, that if you are standing, I'd advise you to sit down." He turned back to the watchman. "Will you tell us all what you told me earlier — what saved you from certain death?"

The watchman milked the moment for all it was worth. It was easy to see that he was trying to look as heroic as possible.

"Normally, I wouldn't have thought twice about going up on the roof alone. But something happened to me this afternoon that made me think twice," he said with a note of drama in his voice.

"Earlier today, a police detective came by. With him was a young woman about seventeen years old. When she saw me, she said she was surprised I was alive because she'd had a vision of me — dead. She said someone was going to push me off this building. She described exactly what this character would look like, too — right down to the shiny medallion he held out as he came at me."

"Incredible!" the newscaster murmured. "Just incredible."

The watchman nodded. "I don't pay any attention to that hocus-pocus garbage. Frankly, I thought she was crazy. But when I heard that noise on the roof, I remembered what she said and picked up a crowbar and took it with me. When he came at me, I struck out with the crowbar a couple times. Then I was able to regain my balance and I took off after him. I guess he didn't expect that, and he got scared."

"So you're sure it was a man that attacked you?"

The watchman's face went blank. "Well, uh," he stammered.

"That's all the time we have," the newscaster cut in. He faced the camera.

"There you have it, folks. A young woman predicted this ghastly attempted murder, and in no small way she helped to prevent it. Young woman, if you're out there, we ask that you come forward and tell us how you knew of this. I'm Mark Wappner, *Channel Ten News*."

There was a commercial break. Cartoon characters sang about a spicy new pet treat called "Taco-Cat." Grayson got to her feet, but her knees buckled. She steadied herself by leaning on the back of the couch. Her head was spinning.

A thought that had been hovering around the edges of her mind thrust itself forward. She knew now why the bridge in her vision had been missing when she'd looked out over the water near the warehouse. The bridge was part of a third murder!

Chapter 14

Finally the sick, spinning sensation went away and Grayson was able to stand up. Gingerly, she took a few steps. Satisfied that she was all right, she walked toward the bathroom to wash her face. On the way, she noticed that the door to Kara's bedroom was closed.

Grayson knocked gently on the door. Then she opened it. Kara's bed was made. On the bedspread lay the sweater she'd forgotten to take to the cleaners the day before. Kara never came home last night, Grayson realized. *Where is she? Why didn't she call?*

She went back to the living room to call Kara's office. The light on the telephone answering machine was flashing. She pressed the playback button and listened.

"Hi, Grayson, it's Kara. I'm working late again, and it looks like I'm not going to be done

*until nearly midnight. I'm going to stay over-
night with Jenny. She works with me, and she
only lives a few blocks from the office. I'll call
you tomorrow. 'Bye. Oh — I almost forgot. Tell
the super to look at the faucet in the kitchen
sink. It keeps dripping. 'Bye."*

There was a beep that signaled the end of
the message. I'd love to get the super to fix
the faucet, but I've banged on his door at least
five times and he's never there, thought Grayson. She was wondering why Kara hadn't left
Jenny's phone number when another beep signaled the beginning of a second message.

*"This is a message for Grayson Dean. Gray-
son, this is Frank Soames. I hope you can come
down to the precinct today. We have to talk. It's
important."*

A beep signaled the end of the second message. Grayson heard the whirring sound of the
tape rewinding. You're right, detective, she
thought. We've got a lot to talk about.

Across the desk, Detective Soames looked
at Grayson solemnly. "You were right about
the attempt on the watchman."
Grayson twisted a little in her chair. "I

know. I saw him on the news. I'll tell you something else. I don't think I had a vision of two murders. I think it was *three*." She told him what she thought about the view of the bridge in her last vision.

The detective nodded thoughtfully. "You could be right. The view from the warehouse looks over the Hudson River. The bridges are over the East River, on the other side of Manhattan. You can see those bridges from loads of places in Brooklyn and Manhattan. I wish we had more to go on."

Grayson slammed her fist on the desk. "Having these visions is awful. I know the killer will try again, and I'm powerless to do anything about it because I don't have enough information."

The detective swallowed. "That's the way we all feel. We just have to keep trying."

Grayson bit her lip. "This is beginning to scare me, more and more. What if the watchman had known my name? He probably would have told everyone right there on television. The killer would know who I was — and probably come after me."

Detective Soames took off his glasses and looked at her. "We're not going to let that happen. I've given the word to everyone in the precinct that they're not to say a word to anyone — not their husbands, wives, children, not even their *pets*. No one. You'd better do your part and do the same."

A guilty recollection of last night's conversation with Jared passed through Grayson's mind. She decided not to tell the detective. Jared had said he hated being associated with the case. He wouldn't appreciate it if she got him involved. Besides, he certainly wasn't the killer.

"I haven't told anyone about my visions except you and Detective Lawson, and my doctor."

"Your doctor?"

"I told you about that already," Grayson said. "He's my eye doctor, and the visions started right after the transplant, so naturally, when I went for the checkup, I told him about it."

"Oh. Of course. That's all right. But don't mention a word to anyone else — not your sister or your boyfriend, or your friends."

Grayson looked away. "Nobody."

"Okay. I've got something to show you." Detective Soames walked over to a file cabinet. When he was gone, Grayson picked up his pen and held it between her hands.

She could feel the detective's energy the same way she had felt Jared's when he touched her hand. Detective Soames was consumed with this case; she could sense it. She could sense something else, too. Something that made her lips curve into a smile.

The detective returned, carrying a folder. "Could I have my pen back, please?" he said as he sat down. "And would you please tell me what you're smiling about?"

"Sure." Grayson laughed. "Did you have a pint of chocolate marshmallow ice cream for breakfast?"

Detective Soames raised his eyebrows. "As a matter of fact, I did." He tilted his head toward her. "You sensed that from touching my pen." It was a statement rather than a question.

Grayson nodded. "It's the kind of thing that's started happening just recently."

"It's called psychometry," Detective Soames said. "Aileen Mills was very good at it. She could touch someone's jewelry and tell you about their whole life."

Grayson looked into his eyes. "You were in love with her," she said. "I could hear it in your voice just now."

"She wasn't in love with me," the detective said after a moment.

"I'm sorry."

"It's all in the past." He shrugged. Clearing

his throat, he opened a file folder. Once more he was all business.

"Aileen used to be able to tell a great deal from photographs. She said she didn't understand how it worked, but she could look at photos and tell things about the subject.

"I'm going to show you some photos of Zeke Stuart. Look at them, touch them, and see if you pick up any information. Perhaps Stuart knew the killer, or found out something about him before he died."

He handed her a folder with photos in plastic sleeves. "Here are the pictures. I'm going to grab a cup of coffee. I'll see you when I get back."

"Okay," Grayson agreed. She began running her hands over the photos as she looked at them. She waited for some sensation to come.

Soon it did, like heat seeping into her skin. Zeke Stuart appeared flamboyant. He had an arrogant side, but there was also a part that was scared and insecure. He couldn't believe that all this wealth had come to him and that he was going to get to keep it.

He didn't keep it for long, she thought. He was killed. She kept looking at photos, and touching them. She didn't learn much more about Zeke Stuart, and she didn't find anything that linked him to a killer.

Grayson turned to another page of photos. What she saw riveted her. It was a picture of Zeke Stuart dressed in a tuxedo, evidently at some sort of party. He and another man were clicking glasses in a toast, laughing. The other man was Dr. Leeds.

Chapter 15

Grayson stuffed the picture of Dr. Leeds and Zeke Stuart into her purse. She didn't wait for Detective Soames to return. She left the police station without saying a word to anyone.

She walked briskly, without a backward glance, until she was several blocks away from the police station. Then she called Dr. Leeds from a public phone. Her appointment wasn't scheduled for several days, but she pleaded an emergency.

Half an hour later, she sat across from Dr. Leeds in his office. He listened quietly, his hands clasped on his desk, as Grayson told him about working with the police.

"Why didn't you tell me you knew Zeke Stuart?" she asked. "I told you I had visions of his murder and you acted as if you hardly remembered the man's name. What are you hiding?"

Dr. Leeds's flat gray eyes stared back at her calmly. "I didn't know Zeke Stuart."

"Yes you *did!*"

Dr. Leeds tapped his pen on the desk. "Grayson, you're hysterical. Your involvement with this case is disturbing and unhealthy. I'm sorry that you have been encouraged in this preposterous idea of psychic visions."

"But I told you, when I gave the detective the name of the donor for my cornea transplant, he told me she was a psychic who worked with the police! Can't you see that it makes sense that I've picked up her psychic ability?"

In a rare display of emotion, Dr. Leeds slammed his hand flat on the desk. "It doesn't make any sense *whatsoever*. The whole idea of psychics is nonsense. The thing they do isn't a *science*. It's something akin to gypsy fortune-telling and those telephone hot lines."

Grayson fished in her bag and pulled out the picture of Zeke Stuart and Dr. Leeds. She handed it to the doctor. "If you didn't know Zeke Stuart, then how do you explain *this*?" she asked accusingly.

The doctor looked at the picture. His expression changed to one of surprise. "Well

— so there we are after all. I didn't even remember that picture."

He stroked his chin thoughtfully. Then he snapped his fingers. "I remember now! This was taken at a fund-raiser five years ago. Everyone was toasting to how much money was raised, and we clicked glasses." Dr. Leeds put the photograph down. "The man and I were at the same fund-raiser, that's all. I told you — I don't know him."

Grayson took back the picture and glared at Dr. Leeds with a look of stubborn suspicion. She smoothed the picture with her hand. For the first time, it registered on her that it was from a magazine.

Grayson realized that she'd been so shocked to see Dr. Leeds and Zeke Stuart in a picture together, she'd switched onto automatic pilot. She hadn't given the slightest thought to why Dr. Leeds's picture would appear in a magazine. Now she began to read the paragraphs beside the picture.

The article's headline was torn off, but it didn't take Grayson long to discover that what the doctor had said was true. "This picture was taken at a fund-raiser for research on eye diseases," she whispered.

Dr. Leeds nodded. "Let me show you

something." He went to a closet and came back with a stack of framed photographs. "My mother keeps telling me to put these up in the office. She keeps telling me to do a lot of things." He smiled. "It seems too ostentatious, though." He put the stack of photos on the desk. "Go ahead. Have a look."

Slowly, Grayson picked up the first photo. There was Dr. Leeds with a well-known opera singer. She picked up the next photograph. There he was with a famous baseball player. Grayson kept going through the pictures, picking up photo after photo of Dr. Leeds with celebrities and politicians.

"You didn't have any idea I was so famous, did you?" he asked. "Well, I'm not. I'm connected with a lot of charities, and I'm active in public affairs. All these photos were taken at events of one kind or another. Some of those people I got to know. Some of them I didn't."

"I see," Grayson said quietly, feeling embarrassed.

"Now, since you're here, we may as well examine your eyes. At least this appointment won't be a total waste of time."

Wordlessly, Grayson took a seat in the examination chair.

"Your progress is really quite remarkable,"

Dr. Leeds said as he checked her eyes. "I've never seen anything quite like it. I thought you might be ready for glasses or contact lenses, but it appears that you won't need them."

Grayson smiled.

"Such an amazing improvement in such a short time," the doctor murmured, as if to himself. He shook his head. "Well, that wraps it up for today. I'll see you in a few weeks. My secretary is out to lunch, so you can phone for an appointment." Dr. Leeds went to his desk and began jotting down notes.

"I'm sorry I accused you of lying," Grayson said when she reached the door. Dr. Leeds didn't look up from what he was writing. It seemed that he didn't even hear her.

When Grayson got home, she banged on the super's door. Once again, no one was home. What good is having a super if he's never around to fix anything, she asked herself as she headed upstairs.

Inside the apartment, she checked the answering machine. The only message was from Kara, who said she was working late that night.

"Again?" Grayson asked the empty apartment. She was beginning to worry about her sister's obsession with getting ahead at work. Kara looked tired lately. She had dark circles under her eyes that she hid with makeup. Grayson decided she'd say something to her about it — if Kara was ever around long enough.

She thought about renting a movie, but then dialed Mina's number instead. Mina picked up on the third ring.

"Grayson! How are you?" she bubbled enthusiastically. Without waiting for an answer, she went on talking. "I heard through the grapevine that Jared likes you a lot. So — are you doing anything tonight?"

"That's why I called you," Grayson said quickly, when Mina paused for air. "I was wondering what you were up to."

"I don't have any plans. I was looking forward to being bored to tears. Want to go to a movie? There's a new thriller playing at the theater up the block."

"Oh, yeah. The one about the werewolf."

"We could go for pizza after."

"Okay. What time is it playing?"

"I'll check. Hold on."

There was a faint click as Mina put the receiver down. In a moment she was back. Grayson heard the rattling of the newspaper. "The

97

movie starts at seven forty-five. I'll stop by your house at seven-fifteen, and we can walk over together."

"Great!"

The movie was so good that Grayson didn't mind that it was three hours long. Afterward they walked down Seventh Avenue to Mina's favorite pizza place.

"So, how's it going with Jared?" Mina asked as they carried their slices to the table.

Grayson took a bite of her pizza and shrugged.

"What does that mean?" Mina asked with raised eyebrows. She mimicked Grayson's shrug.

"Hey, Mina!" a voice called out. Mina looked up and waved. Two guys and a girl waved back and headed toward their table.

Grayson was glad for the interruption. She would have liked to confide in Mina, but she knew if she started talking about Jared, she would end up pouring out the whole story, including the part about being psychic and having visions of murder.

"This is Steve, Craig, and Mary Lee," Mina introduced her friends to Grayson. They all ate pizza and talked and laughed for a long time.

When Grayson got home, it was very late. The street was quiet and still. Grayson heard the sound of her own footsteps echoing on the concrete as she ran up the steps.

She opened the front door and stepped inside, trying not to make any noise. She walked slowly upstairs, wincing as she heard them squeak. It was a deafening sound in the building's sleepy silence.

As she crept down the hallway, she fished in her bag for her keys. I hope there is a message from Jared, she thought.

Nearing her apartment, Grayson noticed something lying on the rug just outside the door. Even before she could tell what it was, she could feel the heat of the rage radiating from it. She slowed her steps.

It was a newspaper. WAREHOUSE WATCHMAN SAVED FROM DEATH BY PSYCHIC, blared the headline. Over the story that followed, a message was slashed in an angry red scrawl. I KNOW WHO YOU ARE AND I'M WATCHING YOU. DON'T SPOIL MY PLANS AGAIN, OR YOU'LL BE NEXT!

Chapter 16

Grayson dropped the newspaper and brought her hand toward her mouth. She whirled around, half-expecting someone to leap out at her.

When she had reassured herself that she was alone in the hallway, Grayson bent down to pick up the newspaper. She stopped short at the sight of the red slash across her palm and the red stain on the front of her shirt.

It took a moment for her shock to subside. Then she realized that the red was not blood. It had come from the red writing on the newspaper.

Slowly, Grayson rubbed her finger across the red scrawl. It smeared. She looked at it carefully. It's lipstick, she realized.

Grayson pulled a Kleenex from her bag and wiped the lipstick off her hand. Then she picked up the newspaper again. She went inside the apartment and double-locked the door behind her.

Leaning against the door, Grayson read the newspaper story through the angry red scrawls. It didn't reveal anything more than the news program had. There was no mention of her name or address, or even a physical description beyond the fact that she was a young woman about seventeen years old. How had the killer found her?

Maybe it wasn't the killer after all, Grayson thought. She looked at the angry message, and the wheels in her mind started turning. Who knew that she was the psychic the watchman talked about, and was sick enough to pull a prank like this?

Still holding the newspaper, Grayson's hands began trembling uncontrollably. The walls begin to ripple before her eyes. She tried to let go of the newspaper, but she was unable to make it fall from her grasp. There was an overpowering energy coming from it, reaching out to her, pulling her under.

Grayson felt herself being swept into the vision. The apartment vanished from her eyes. Suddenly she was standing in semidarkness. Outside the opaque window, she could see the flashing of neon signs.

She looked around. There was dust everywhere. What was this place?

Her eyes began to adjust to the darkness. When will the killer appear? she asked herself, looking around warily.

That's when she saw *them*. They took her breath away as they stood together, staring at her with cold, glittering eyes, as stiff and pale as corpses.

Some of them had no arms. Some had no legs. Some still stared through the darkness even though their heads were no longer attached to their bodies.

Her heart raced. They're mannequins, she realized. They looked like deathly, ghoulish creatures.

This was a department store, but this floor wasn't in use. It was being worked on, or perhaps used for storage.

Grayson listened for the sound of footsteps. Her ears strained for the slightest noise. She knew there was someone here.

Then she heard the squeak, squeak, squeak of rubber soles on the tile. He came creeping round the corner, swinging a flashlight in a jaunty manner but looking around nervously. Another man in uniform, Grayson thought to herself as he came into view. He must be the security guard. Grayson felt herself entering his mind, his thoughts.

His fear engulfed her. *He's scared because he knows about the murder attempt at the warehouse, and he's afraid something will happen to him. But he's trying to be brave.*

Pull back, she told herself. She remembered that Detective Soames had told her she could learn to pull back and step *beside* the vision. That way she could see more. If she got too close, she would be overcome by the victim's fear. She might even feel the victim's pain.

Grayson forced herself to relax and float, float away from the man's mind. The moment she was free, she began to look around for the killer. But something grabbed her and drew her in with a hard, slamming force, as if she were being drawn into the eye of a tornado.

She tried to pull away again, but the force was too strong — and too horrible. Something sick with rage and fear had gotten hold of her.

I'm inside the killer's mind.

Grayson was held powerless in the mind of the killer as the killer crept up behind the frightened young security guard. He was standing in front of an open elevator shaft. He never heard the killer behind him.

Then he was falling. His terror was like an

explosion of fireworks before Grayson's eyes.

Grayson felt a flash of the killer's twisted glee. And then — abruptly — the sick mind released her.

Her heart pounding, she found herself standing in the kitchen again. The newspaper had fallen from her hand.

Grayson looked at it as if it were a monster. The vision she had seen had come from touching it. The message was no prank — the killer had written it. The killer was watching her.

I can't think about that now, Grayson thought, clenching her fists. She prayed that the murder she had just seen hadn't happened yet. A look at the clock told her that it was half-past midnight. The lateness of the hour didn't matter. She hurried to the phone and dialed Detective Soames's home phone number. The telephone rang and rang and rang, but there was no answer.

Chapter 17

Half an hour after she made the first call to Detective Soames's house, Grayson picked up the phone to call again. She was about to press the first number, when her hand stopped in midair.

What am I thinking of, she asked herself. Frank said he'd be working night and day on this case. He's probably at the precinct right now.

Quickly, Grayson dialed the detective's number at the police station. She felt a wave of relief when she heard his voice on the other end of the line.

"Detective Soames, this is Grayson Dean. It's happened again."

The detective didn't have to ask what she was talking about. He knew. "What did you see?" he barked.

He barely gave Grayson time to get the

story out before telling her he had to get to work on it. I didn't even get a chance to tell him about the message on the newspaper, she thought. There would be time enough for that, though.

What worried her was whether the half-hour between phone calls had cost a man his life. I'll never be able to sleep until I know that someone else didn't become another victim tonight, she thought.

But in spite of her fears, weariness overtook her moments later. She was barely able to make it to her room before her eyes closed. Fully clothed, she threw herself across her bed and slept.

"Grayson, wake up. There's someone on the phone for you. A Detective Soames."

Grayson opened her eyes to see Kara staring down at her. She was dressed in a pinkish-gray jacket and matching slacks. "Why did you fall asleep with your clothes on?" she asked.

Grayson sat up. "Why are you dressed for work? It's Saturday."

"I asked you first, but never mind. I have to go in to the office this weekend. We're having a meeting, and then I've got some work to catch up on. Here, take the call." She held the cordless telephone out to Grayson.

Great, Grayson thought, as she took the telephone from her sister's hand. Now Kara will want to know what's going on.

She heard Detective Soames's voice on the other end of the line. "Did I catch you before you've seen the morning paper?"

"Ummm . . . yes," Grayson said sleepily.

"Well, then, listen to this. It's all over the headlines. You were right on the money about the attempted murder. I dispatched teams to the major department stores. We got to the right one just in time."

"What happened?" Grayson was wide awake now, sitting up in bed. She saw that Kara was hovering in the doorway, making no attempt to disguise her curiosity.

"The killer pushed a young security guard into an open elevator shaft. The kid managed to grab onto a cable as he fell. He couldn't have held on much longer, though. We got there just in time. Thanks to you, he's going to be all right."

Grayson realized that she had been holding her breath and exhaled.

"I can't stand this much longer. What if you hadn't been able to find him in time? How do you think I could live with that? What about next time?"

She could feel the tension in Detective

Soames's voice as he spoke. "What we've got to do is catch the murderer before there *is* a next time. I've got an idea that may help us. Can you get down here to the station soon?"

"Of course. I'll get there as soon as I can." Grayson reached for her robe as she hung up.

"Not so fast," Kara said as Grayson headed for the bathroom. "A detective calls, and then, in an instant, you're practically out the door." Kara crossed her arms and looked at Grayson sternly. "What's going on?"

Grayson's gaze wavered as she looked into her sister's eyes. "It's nothing I want to bother you with, Kara. You've got enough to think about, and you seem so tense and tired lately. Do you think you might be working too hard?"

"Don't try to change the subject!" Kara snapped. "Worrying about what you might be involved in isn't going to make me any less tense or help me concentrate on my job. Out with it."

Detective Soames had told her to keep quiet, but one look at Kara's face told Grayson that she'd have to let her sister know the truth. "Maybe you'd better sit down, Kara," she began. "This is going to be a big shock."

When Grayson was finished with her story, Kara looked at her and said, "It's a pretty fantastic tale, Grayson."

Grayson nodded. "Believe me, I *know* how fantastic it sounds. Up until a few weeks ago, I wouldn't have believed it myself. But after what has happened, I do now."

"You know I want what's best for you, Grayson." Kara's voice sounded brittle. "This whole thing has me worried." Grayson was surprised to see Kara's eyes flash with anger. "Frankly, I've been worried too often about you already. It's been distracting me at work, and I don't need that." Kara stopped speaking abruptly and took a deep breath. "I'm sorry. I didn't mean what I just said."

Grayson was stunned. She had no idea that Kara felt any resentment toward her.

"I guess I haven't thought about how much you had to do for me," said Grayson.

"It's not that I minded doing it, Grayson. I've just been worried about you all through the operations. You're staying with me in New York City, and if anything ever happened to you, Mom and Dad would never forgive me. I'd never forgive myself."

Grayson laid a hand on her sister's shoulder. "Nothing's going to happen to me, Kara."

Kara got to her feet. "I don't want you to have anything more to do with this murder case. It's dangerous. This character is vicious and unstable. Besides, I'm inclined to agree with what Dr. Leeds told you, no matter how wrong you think he is. I think this psychic hocus-pocus is nonsense, and this detective who is encouraging you is being extremely irresponsible."

"But Kara, you heard how I saved two people from being killed."

Kara picked up her purse. "It's some kind of weird coincidence." She turned to leave. "I've got to go to work. You're not fooling around with these predictions anymore, and that's final!" She left without another word.

When she was gone, Grayson sat very still, thinking. What Kara said was true. Her involvement with the murder case *was* dangerous.

The killer knew where she lived, and probably wasn't happy about last night's thwarted murder attempt. Detective Soames's words echoed in her mind. *We've got to catch the killer before there is a next time.* That's what I've got to help him do, she told herself. Then she went to get dressed.

On her way out she stopped to check the mailbox, then remembered that it was too early for the mail delivery. But something inside the mailbox caught her eye. She opened the little door and took out a piece of paper.

The sentences written on it were practically

illegible, as if whoever wrote it had tried to disguise their handwriting. But Grayson was able to make out what the message was:

DON'T GET IN MY WAY AGAIN. THIS IS THE LAST WARNING.

Grayson dropped the piece of paper as if it had scorched her fingers. The instant she'd done so, she realized she should show it to Detective Soames. As she bent down to pick it up, she saw a pen on the floor in the corner of the vestibule. She looked at it closely.

The letters on the pen were easy to see. They formed the monogram KMD. Grayson recognized the pen. It was Kara's.

Chapter 18

Grayson held Kara's pen in front of her, her mind numbed with shock. Soon, however, her lips curved into a smile.

Kara wrote that note to scare me away from the case, she thought. It's just the kind of trick she used to do when we were kids, like telling me there were rats in her room so I wouldn't go in there. Well, we're not kids anymore, and you can't fool me, Kara. She slipped the pen into her pocket. Still smiling, she headed for the bus stop.

Headlines screamed at every newsstand about last night's failed murder attempt. Grayson passed by them all without stopping to buy a paper. Her mind was on the newspaper in her bag with the writing scrawled on it. Today she was going to show it to Detective Soames.

At the bus stop, she waited anxiously for a sign of the approaching bus. Then she noticed someone looking at her. It was a short, stout man wearing a loud colored shirt that clashed with his plaid shorts. He kept looking at Grayson and counting on his fingers, from one to five, again and again.

It's nothing, Grayson told herself. He's odd, that's all. Yet her growing nervousness would not permit her to stay there. She began walking toward the subway.

Grayson didn't like the subway, with its dimness and dirt and graffiti. It would take her longer to get to the police station by subway, too. But right now, she didn't care.

As the subway car rattled along from stop to stop, Grayson tried to keep her mind occupied by studying the advertisements that papered the car above the windows. They were advertisements urging people to remove warts, tend to bunions and fallen arches, buy roach motels, and spend the day at the racetrack.

Out of the corner of her eye, she noticed a tall, thin man with a pointed nose sitting across the aisle from her. He kept casting sidelong glances her way. All the while, he drummed his fingers on the seat in front of him, until the woman sitting there asked him to stop.

The man stopped drumming his fingers on

the seat, but he glared angrily at the back of the woman's head. Then he began glancing at Grayson again, moving his lips, whispering something she could not hear.

It's *him*, Grayson thought in a panic. It's the killer. He followed me into the subway.

But the man got off at the next stop. Out the window, Grayson watched him walk down the platform, drumming his fingers on his thigh, glancing to his left every so often, and whispering.

He wasn't really looking at me at all, Grayson thought. He was just doing what he always does. He was just one of those odd people Kara told me are all around big cities. I thought he was the killer because I'm a nervous wreck.

She looked down and saw that her hands were trembling. Pull yourself together, Grayson, she said silently.

By the time she reached the police station, Grayson's hands had stopped shaking. She appeared calm outwardly, but her palms were sweaty as she faced Detective Soames. "You said you had an idea, Frank. What is it?"

"I'd just like to give something a try. One thing we do in murder cases is to get what we call a psychological profile of the killer. We try to learn as much as we can about the person and try to analyze the motivation for the killings. Understand?"

Grayson nodded. "I think so. You want to know things like why the killer picks certain victims. You want to find out if it's connected to something in the killer's past, for instance. That sort of thing."

"You got it. Now, we already know the killer is organized, methodical. The victims were probably staked out for a long time, because the killer knew to strike when the victims would be alone and the killer would be able to get away without being caught. If not for you, the killer would have succeeded in killing two more people."

Grayson felt a chill travel along her spine. "Not necessarily. Something else might have happened to save them."

Detective Soames shrugged. "Not likely, but suit yourself. Anyway, I've already sent some information to the FBI. They have a unit that composes psychological profiles of criminals. But they're bogged down with lots of cases, and it could take some time. I want to move on this character as quickly as possible."

He shoved a folder across the desk. "You've already looked at pictures of Zeke Stuart. Here are some photos of the next two people who almost became victims. Take a look at the pictures and hold them in your hands. See if you get any image at all. What can you learn about these men? What made the killer pick them?"

Grayson took a deep breath. "Okay, let's go." She took the photos out of the folder and spread them out on the desk.

"This one is Charlie Harris, the security guard," Soames said, pointing to a picture of a dark-haired, dark-eyed young man.

Grayson put her hands on the photo and was surprised to feel the energy emanating from it immediately. "He's very ambitious. He's working as a security guard while he's going to school." Grayson's hand on the photograph felt warm. "He's very ambitious," she said again. Something was stirring inside. "He sometimes — isn't very considerate of others' feelings. He's a bit of a bully, and enjoys taunting others and making them feel foolish."

"Try the photos of the watchman," the detective urged. "His name is Fred Hoyt."

Grayson recognized the likeness of the middle-aged watchman from the warehouse. Fred Hoyt was gray-haired with blue eyes. She put her hand on his picture. At first she didn't get anything, but gradually she felt something like a weak, steady current.

"He's not like the other man," she said after a moment. "He's not ambitious at all. In fact, he's lazy. And unlike the other man, he doesn't have a mean streak. He's outgoing and he likes people." She smiled. "He likes to tell jokes."

Grayson pushed the photo away. "These two men don't seem the least bit similar. Maybe the killer just picked them because they worked in places where it was easy to catch them alone, and push them. . . ." Her voice trailed off.

Detective Soames tilted his head to one side thoughtfully. "Maybe that's part of it. Maybe that's all of it, but I don't think so. Let's try something else. Try to see these men as the killer saw them."

Grayson pushed her chair back. "You're asking me to get inside the killer's mind. I've been there already. It's a horrible place."

Detective Soames stared back at her. "We've got to catch this killer."

Grayson swallowed hard. She put one hand on a photo of Frank Hoyt, the other on the photo of Charlie Harris. In a moment, messages began coming. They tumbled over one another. She couldn't make any sense of them. She took her hands away. "It's not working. It's too confusing." She began to get up out of her chair.

"Wait," Detective Soames barked. "Try again. This is important."

Grayson sat down again. "All right, I'll try."

First she laid a hand on Frank Hoyt's picture. She began to get the same information she had when she studied it before. No, no, no, she thought. What does the killer look like? Has the next victim been chosen?

It felt as if her mind had run up against a brick wall. The information was there somewhere, she could feel it — she just couldn't get at it. Her hands began shaking and her head started to hurt. The hurt became a sharp, splitting pain.

Panicking, Grayson pulled back. The pain receded. Ask another question, her mind whispered. Ask . . . *why*.

As the minutes ticked by, Detective Soames tapped his pen nervously on the desk. He was on the verge of shaking Grayson to bring her out of the trance, when she opened her eyes.

"Thank goodness," he said. "I was beginning to think you weren't coming back."

"It was intense," Grayson said. "Could I have a drink of water?"

"Sure." The detective got up and returned with a paper cup full of water. Grayson drank deeply.

"I'm not sure how helpful this will be. I tried

to find out if the killer was male or female, and what he or she looked like. No luck. I also tried to find out about the next victim, and I thought I was getting somewhere — but then I ran up against a kind of wall. It was strange." Grayson gave a little shudder.

"What I did find out is this. There's some problem between the killer and someone in the killer's family. The killer is very angry, and very scared, too. The anger is very powerful, and so is the fear. The reason for killing is to get rid of both the anger and the fear."

Chapter 19

Detective Soames gathered up the pictures. He picked out one of the security guard and one of the watchman and handed them to Grayson. "Hang on to these. Maybe you'll pick up some more information." He leaned his chin on the palm of his hand.

"The killer chooses male victims, so it stands to reason that the problem is with a man — a father, or a brother, perhaps."

Grayson felt uneasiness stirring inside as she remembered Jared's problem with his brother. It's just a coincidence, she told herself.

She reached into her bag and pulled out the newspaper and the other message she'd received. "What about these?" She put them on the desk. Detective Soames examined them with a deepening frown.

"Besides the police, who knows you're working on this case?"

Grayson shifted in her chair. "You told me not to tell anybody."

Detective Lawson chimed in from the next desk. "You told somebody. You kids love to talk. Probably you got into a gab session with the girls and pretty soon blah, blah, blah, you were blabbing away about your psychic work with the police department while your girlfriends oohed and aaahed."

"No, I didn't!" Grayson turned to him furiously.

"Lay off, Lawson, I'm trying to conduct a murder investigation here."

"Ha! Your investigation is a carnival sideshow," Lawson said. But he picked up his coffee cup and wandered away.

Grayson watched him leave. "He doesn't seem to like you much — or me either. Would he do something like this?" She pointed to the messages.

"Lawson?" Detective Soames's eyes widened. "Absolutely not. Detective Lawson may not think much of my methods, but he's not a prankster."

Grayson watched Lawson talking to a clerk, laughing and sneering. "He looks capable of playing some nasty pranks to me," Grayson said doubtfully.

"Well, he's not. Lawson's no charm-school graduate, but he's a professional." He looked Grayson in the eye. "Did you tell one of your girlfriends, Grayson?"

"No!" Grayson cast a sidelong look at Lawson. She leaned across the desk. "I told my sister," she said in a hushed voice.

"You told your sister!" Soames bellowed. All heads in the room turned toward them. Grayson caught a glimpse of Lawson's grinning face.

"I *had to* tell my sister," she hissed. "Kara answered the phone when you called this morning, remember? She wanted to know why a detective was calling me. What was I supposed to do?"

Detective Soames let out a sigh. "I suppose I see what you mean."

Grayson began playing with a ring on her right index finger. She was growing more uncomfortable by the minute.

"So, Grayson, your doctor knows, and your sister knows." He eyed her critically. "Why do I get the feeling that's not the end of the story?"

"My boyfriend," Grayson said softly, keeping her eyes on the ring.

"What about your boyfriend?"

Grayson's voice was barely above a whisper. "I told him I was working on the case."

"Why didn't you tell me this before?"

"I didn't want to get Jared involved," Grayson blurted out. She regretted her words as soon as they were out of her mouth.

The detective looked at her steadily. "Why would he get involved?"

Grayson looked toward the windows. She shrugged. "I don't know."

The detective raised his voice. "You're keeping something from me, and I want to know what it is. Now, let's hear it."

"Okay, okay. Jared has a construction job this summer, and he worked on renovating Zeke Stuart's apartment. I thought that as soon as you found out, you'd want to bring him in for questioning." Grayson looked at the detective earnestly. "Jared doesn't have anything to do with the killings."

"Improbable, maybe. But not impossible."

"No, you don't know Jared. I've been close to him. He's a wonderful person."

"It sounds as if your emotional involvement might get in the way of your psychic talents. That's what happens, you know. Emotional involvement blocks a psychic from getting clear messages. He's your boyfriend, after all."

"I'm not seeing him anymore," Grayson said. "I told him there was too much on my mind with this case going on."

The detective leaned back in his chair. "Okay, you told him about working on the case, and then you said you didn't want to see him anymore. Let's figure it made him mad. He knows where you live." The detective pointed to the angry message scrawled in red. "He could be the one who left this in front of your door, just as a nasty trick to get back at you."

Grayson shook her head. "He wouldn't do that," she said emphatically. She went back to playing with her ring.

"You're probably right, Grayson. Anyway, if the guy worked on the construction crew that renovated Stuart's apartment, I've already talked to him. We had a list of everyone on the crew, and we brought them all in."

Grayson looked up sharply. "Jared didn't say anything about being questioned by the police."

"Well, he must have been. Let's check. What's his name?"

"Jared Moore."

Detective Soames typed Jared's name into

the computer on his desk. He frowned. Then he punched some more keys. And frowned again.

"It seems I haven't seen your boyfriend after all. I checked the names of people who were questioned, and he's not there. Then I checked the list of the members of the construction crew. His name isn't on it."

Chapter 20

Grayson was still shaken by all that had happened at the police station that afternoon when she got home. So what if Jared's name wasn't listed as part of the construction crew, she thought as she opened the front door of the brownstone. It was probably just a mistake. Right now, she was looking forward to going upstairs and taking a long, hot shower.

It felt as if she were dragging her feet up every step. When she got to the landing, she sighed wearily.

As Grayson began walking down the hall, a looming figure stepped out of the shadows. It was a tall, big-boned man with a head of shaggy gray hair. "Who are you?" Grayson asked.

The man acted as if he hadn't heard her. Taking a step toward her, he said, "Now everything is ruined."

For an awful moment, Grayson was unable

to move. The man was holding a hammer in his right hand. He smacked the head lightly against the palm of his left hand.

Before he could come any closer, Grayson turned and ran. She grabbed the banister and began running downstairs as fast as she could.

As she reached the first floor, she started to dash for the front door. Her heart sank as she saw that the chain lock had been fastened. She knew she'd never be able to remove it before the man caught her.

Somehow, she managed to scream. As the sound of her shrieking tore through the air, a door opened and an elderly woman poked her head out.

Grayson ran past the woman into the apartment and slammed the door. The tiny lady stared at her, wide-eyed. She was holding a feather duster in one hand. A kerchief was tied around her head.

"Call the police," Grayson panted. "He's after me!"

The woman's mouth dropped open. Grayson jumped as she heard three loud thumps at the door.

"It's me, Degan, Mrs. Kaminsky. Please open up."

Grayson shook her head from side to side. "No, no! Don't open the door."

The woman gave her a reassuring smile. "Don't worry, dear. It's only Degan. I know his voice."

With a strange, off-balance feeling of confusion, Grayson watched as the woman put down the feather duster and opened the door. "What's all the excitement about, Degan?" she asked, as the man walked into the apartment. "This girl is terrified and pale as a ghost."

The big man shrugged. "I don't know. I was waiting for someone to come home so that I could have a look at the bathroom tiles. She saw me and took off running. I'm not that scary-looking, am I?" A smile spread over his face.

"You're the super?" Grayson asked. But she'd already figured out the answer.

"Well, I'm sure not a movie star," the man said. "Didn't your sister tell you she asked me to go in and fix the tiles in the bathroom?"

"I guess she forgot."

Degan shook his head. "She should have told you. Then you wouldn't have gotten such a scare. Let's shake hands and start over."

"Sure." Grayson extended her hand. "I'm Grayson." As she shook Degan's hand, Grayson tuned in to his energy. She felt steadiness and quiet. He's a man who leads a simple life, she thought. A regular routine makes him feel content. There's nothing fearful about him.

"I really went off the deep end, I guess," Grayson said. "It's all the stuff about the killer . . . in the papers. To find a stranger in the house . . ."

"Of course!" Degan nodded his head emphatically. His mouth set into a grim line. "That man's a menace."

"Yes, yes. It's so terrible," Mrs. Kaminsky clucked.

"I'd like to get hold of him and teach him a lesson," growled Degan. He touched his index finger to his temple. "He's got to be a real sicko." Then he cocked his head toward Grayson. "He always picks on male victims, you know."

"I know." Grayson shrugged. She wasn't about to explain the reason for her fear. "I wouldn't rule out the possibility that he might change his choice of victims."

Mrs. Kaminsky chuckled. "Degan's not going to throw you out of a window, dear. That's not his style."

The comment struck Grayson as odd. She looked at Mrs. Kaminsky's smiling face, wondering for the first time if the lady was quite "all there." Then she turned to Degan. "You referred to the killer as 'he,' but they don't know if it's a male or female."

Degan gave a dismissive wave of his hand. "Oh, come on. It's got to be a 'he.'" Then he stroked his chin. "Well, now, come to think of it, they did say they didn't know. But I think it's a 'he.'"

He rubbed his palms together briskly. "Let's get back to business. You girls keep letting the water run out over the top of the tub and soak the tiles. It ruins the floor in the bathroom. I guess you haven't been here long enough to blame — but I know your sister's guilty. I'm going to have to regrout most of the tiles on the bathroom floor." He pointed a finger at Grayson. "You watch that that sister of yours doesn't let the tub run over. Don't you do it either!"

Grayson shook her head. "We'll be careful. I promise. Do you want to come back and start your work? I won't run away from you."

Degan laughed. "Okay."

While Degan worked on the floor, Grayson watched television and talked to him. She wanted to take her mind off thoughts of the killer. But after Degan left, the television wasn't enough to occupy her mind.

She took the envelope containing the pictures of the watchman and the security guard from her bag. Opening it, she took the pictures out and sat down on the throw rug in the middle of the living-room floor. She put the pictures on the rug. Then she placed her hand on the one of the watchman and waited.

Images started coming almost immediately. She saw a deserted stairwell, a wall of concrete blocks, an unshaded lightbulb. Then she felt a sickening jolt. The images vanished and she was spinning around and around as she fell into a black void.

With another sickening jolt, she stopped falling and landed with a force that knocked the wind out of her. She went running through the emptiness.

She could feel the rage radiating from the figure that was chasing after her. She felt the heat of a twisted, vicious mind.

Pull back! Pull back! Grayson told herself. She wanted to step beside the victim in the vision, and look at the victim's face. But no matter how she tried, she remained entangled, unable to pull away.

The victim's fear began to overwhelm her. It seeped into her every pore and wrapped itself around her heart. She started to choke.

Suddenly there was an explosion of light in her head that blotted out the vision. Grayson opened her eyes and saw the pattern on the throw rug.

Sitting on the living-room floor, she hugged

her knees to her chest and rocked back and forth. I know why that vision was different, she thought. I know why it was so scary, because I know who the next victim will be.

It's me.

Chapter 21

Grayson felt cold all over. She shivered, and her teeth made clicking sounds as they chattered. She felt too cold even to move.

Finally she managed to stretch her stiff limbs and scramble to her feet. Bent over and hugging herself with her arms, she shuffled toward the bathroom. There she turned on the shower and waited for the water to heat up.

She glanced at her face in the mirror and gasped. The face that stared back at her was drained of color and white as a corpse. Her lips were tinged with blue. I look like I'm already dead, she thought. That's how I feel, too.

Her teeth chattered harder. I had two visions of murders that never were carried out, and the one I've just seen won't be, either, she told herself. Somehow, I'll figure out what to do.

Right now, Grayson just wanted to feel alive again. She jumped into the hot shower and stood there, letting the warm, steady stream flow over her body. Then she picked up her washcloth and lathered it with soap. She scrubbed herself all over again and again until she could feel her body warming up.

Grayson forced herself to make her mind a blank. She thought of nothing but the feeling of warmth that was returning to her body.

She had been in the hot shower for nearly half an hour before she felt alive again. Afterward, she dried off quickly and wrapped herself in a large, fluffy towel. She went to her room and dressed in jeans and a shirt before heading back to the kitchen for a cup of tea.

Cup in hand, she sat down at the kitchen table. Now I'll think of what I should do next, she told herself. Staring into the cloud of steam that rose from the hot tea, she felt a whisper of panic inside.

Should I try to read the photographs of the security guard and the watchman together again? she asked herself. Maybe this time I'll get a look at the killer's face.

The whisper of panic grew stronger and stronger, threatening to overwhelm her. She put the cup down, spilling some of the tea on the table. Her gaze darted around the kitchen walls.

It was impossible to keep calm enough to form a plan. When she imagined having another vision, the idea of getting close to the killer again filled her with terror. She couldn't think of anything else to do, except run and run and run.

I've got to call Detective Soames and tell him what I've seen, Grayson said to herself as she jumped to her feet.

She had started to pick up the handset of the wall phone when a glint of something gold on the floor under the cabinet below the sink caught her eye. She bent down to see what it was.

A lipstick . . . is it mine? she wondered as she picked it up. It didn't look like any that she owned. It must be Kara's, she thought, as she removed the cap to check the color. Inside the tube, the blood-red lipstick was mis-shapen and broken.

The image of the newspaper with the angry red message slashed across it jumped into Grayson's mind. Her insides lurched. No — it can't be. Not Kara.

Holding the lipstick out in front of her, Grayson's hand began to shake. Terrifying rage came through the object and bombarded her — *so dark, so twisted, so vicious.* Pictures burst into her mind, one after the other, like flashbulbs popping — images of bodies falling through the air in endless flight.

But the flight will end, she told herself, letting go of the lipstick. It will end in death.

Grayson leaned against the kitchen counter, trembling. I can't believe Kara is a killer, she thought. But that's what I felt when I picked up her lipstick . . . the murderous rage of a killer . . . the mind of someone insane.

I've got to get out of here.

But it was too late for Grayson to get away. She heard a rattling sound and looked toward the door. Frozen, Grayson could only stare as the door slowly opened.

"You," she breathed.

Chapter 22

"Detective Soames, what's going on?" Grayson asked. "How did you get in here?" She eyed him warily.

An odd little smile spread over his face. "I picked the lock. It's a little trick I learned during my years on the force. It comes in handy sometimes." He shrugged. "I had to talk to you. I had a hunch you finally figured out who the killer is."

Grayson took a step backward. Her mind churned furiously. "Uh — no." She didn't like the strange look on the detective's face.

He picked the lock to get in this time, she thought. Maybe he's gotten in that way before, when he got hold of Kara's lipstick and used it to write that message on the newspaper. *It's possible.*

"I think it would help if we went back to the warehouse," she said. Her eyes flickered from the detective's face to the open door behind him. "Could we go now?" She attempted a smile.

The detective's smile vanished. "Grayson, what's the matter? You seem so nervous," he said in a hushed voice.

"It's n-nothing," she stammered. "I'm fine."

Detective Soames tilted his head to one side. "I can't get over it. I was sitting at my desk and *boom*! Out of the blue I just got such a strong feeling, and I said to myself, Grayson knows, all right. She knows who the killer is."

Grayson took another step backward. *Think!* She told herself furiously. She swallowed. Then a thought hit her. Of course! He wants me to think it's Kara. That's why he used her lipstick to write the message, and then left it here for me to find.

She pointed to the lipstick that was still lying on the floor where she had dropped it.

"I found that. When I picked it up, I had the most terrifying visions. I know that the killer wrote the message with it." She swallowed. "It's Kara's. That means my sister is the killer. I didn't want to tell you. I didn't want to believe it."

Grayson watched the glitter go out of the detective's eyes. "Grayson, I'm so sorry. I know you don't want to believe it's your sister.

I don't want to, either." He stuffed his hands into his pockets. "We'll just wait until she gets home."

Grayson stared as if hypnotized as she saw a movement in the hallway. She heard a thud, and then, as if in slow motion, the detective collapsed the way a marionette does when the puppeteer lets go of the strings.

It all took place so quickly that she didn't realize what had happened. Then she saw the medallion with the lion on it.

Where am I? was the first thought that limped into Grayson's mind when she regained consciousness. Her head hurt terribly.

She remembered the handkerchief being held over her nose and the sharp odor when she breathed. It must have been chloroform, she thought, putting her hands to her head.

She rolled over and sat up. She had been lying on a floor covered with dust. She coughed.

The light from a flashing neon sign filtered dimly through the grime on the windows. In the darkness, Grayson could barely make out her surroundings. She discovered that she was in a huge room divided into row upon row of cages, all made from the same material as a chain-link fence.

She pushed on the door of the cage that held her. It didn't budge. Then she saw that it was held shut by a padlock and chain.

Icy fingers of fear gripped her heart. What kind of place is this? she asked herself, feeling a lump of terror lodge in her throat.

In a flash of understanding, Grayson knew. This is a warehouse, she whispered aloud. These aren't cages, they're storage bins. They all seem to be empty, though.

"This building is abandoned," a voice called from the shadows. "There won't be anyone to disturb us."

Grayson whirled and looked in the direction of the voice. The shadows were too deep. She couldn't see anyone.

"I didn't want to hurt you," the voice went on, "but you've been spoiling my plans for far too long."

Now the voice was whining, like a pouting child.

"But it will still be fun to see you fall." There was no mistaking the sparkle of excitement.

The figure stepped out of the shadows.

"I'm going to watch you falling down and down and down." The voice grew hard and cold. "Then I'll stop feeling sick. That's what happens, you see. The memories start to haunt me, and then the voice comes back to me, teasing and taunting. 'Go ahead,' it says. 'See if you can do anything to me. You can't because I'm too big and you're too small.' "

"Who teased you?" Grayson asked softly. "Who was too big? One of your parents?"

"Not my parents!" The voice barked so angrily that Grayson jumped. "It was my brother. My *step*brother." The voice shook with rage. My parents died, and he took care of me. Ha!" The laugh was brittle and bitter. "His way of talking to me was to torment me."

The figure moved out of the shadows and came toward Grayson. "He used to like to scare me. Before I could swim, he liked to dangle me over the edge of the pool in the deep end. Or he'd hold me over the edge of the balcony in his apartment."

The neon sign flashed, and a spark of light shone on the medallion around the shadowy figure's neck. Grayson couldn't take her eyes off it.

"You're looking at my medallion. It was my father's, and I kept it to remember him by, until my stepbrother took it from me."

Now the voice was shaking. "That night I took it back while he was sleeping. He probably never even missed it. Then I ran away.

"I always wanted him to know I took the medallion back. Then he'd understand that I beat him in the end.

"Years later, the first time I started to feel sick, I tried to find him. If I could have just pushed him off the roof, I think I would have been all right. The sickness would have gone away — the horrible nightmares and the headaches. But I had to make other arrangements."

There was an insane high-pitched tittering.

"After I realized I wasn't going to find my stepbrother, I was in despair. The nightmares were so bad, I couldn't sleep at all, and my insides were so knotted up I couldn't eat. I didn't leave my apartment for days. People kept calling me to fix things until I stopped answering the phone. When I stopped answering the phone, they started banging on the door. I never answered.

"Then one day I saw Zeke Stuart on a talk show. As soon as he walked out onto the stage, I knew that he would help me get over my sickness.

"He walked just like my stepbrother Jake. There was even something about the way he cocked his head to one side that was just like my stepbrother."

The edge of excitement crept back into the voice. "It was amazing. The more I watched him, the more and more he reminded me of my stepbrother. And then — he *became* my stepbrother. I knew that if I could kill Zeke Stuart — kill him the right way, I would find peace once more."

The voice was raving now. It was as if Grayson wasn't even there and the killer was just talking to get the words out.

"It was lucky that ol' Stuart kept talking about his new luxury apartment. It was easy to find where it was. Who would think that the man's number would be listed in the telephone book?

"By the time I picked the lock and got into his apartment, I knew that Zeke Stuart *was* my brother Jake. Oh, he'd changed his name and the way he looked, but it was him all right. Oh — when I saw him fall, what peace I felt!"

The killer was silent. For a moment, Grayson was afraid his story was finished and his mind would turn to killing her. But thankfully, he went on, this time in a voice filled with sadness.

"I thought my torment was ended, but it wasn't. After only a few peaceful days, the sickness began again. I knew that Zeke Stuart wasn't my stepbrother after all — he'd only been a substitute. I'd have to find another one to make the sickness go away."

The killer's voice turned menacing. "I found him, too — that watchman would have been perfect. He had that same little bantam-rooster walk."

The killer took another step. Now he stood outside the storage bin that held Grayson prisoner. "You spoiled it all. You took it away from me. I couldn't imagine who it was — and then I heard you through the vent." He laughed. "I knew you were wondering how I found out. The vents in that old brownstone are incredible. You wouldn't believe the things I've heard.

"Anyhow — I just couldn't believe that psychic story. At first I thought you were just crazy."

You thought I was crazy. For a moment Grayson had a wild impulse to burst out laughing. The impulse passed as she listened to the killer talking on and on.

"Then I went into the apartment and used your sister's lipstick to write that message on the newspaper. . . ." His voice trailed off for a moment.

"Why am I explaining things to you, Grayson? You won't be around to think about them."

He took a key from his pocket and unlocked the padlock. Then he removed the chain and threw it on the floor. "It's time to visit the roof." He chuckled. "There's a lovely view."

"Degan, don't!" Grayson said desperately. "Killing more people won't ever make the sickness go away. It will keep coming back. You need help."

"Help?" the killer whispered. "Degan doesn't need any help. He's fine. But Degan's not here right now. I'm Roy."

Chapter 23

"Degan doesn't know about Roy," the killer said, gripping Grayson's arm tighter and propelling her toward the stairs. "But Roy knows about Degan."

Grayson stumbled along the filthy corridor. She was trying to keep calm enough to think clearly. It was working . . . so far.

"Degan's an okay guy, but he's boring," the killer continued. "He's not fun like I am. But I've got to keep Degan around because he's got that super's job, and I like to eat. I wouldn't care to have a job myself." He chuckled. "Especially not that one."

He's got multiple personalities, Grayson thought, as they reached the stairs. If only there was a way to bring Degan out.

"Come on, now, don't dawdle," Roy said, pulling her roughly.

Grayson went up step after step.

Each step I take brings me closer to the roof and closer to death, she thought. The air in the building was hot and seemed to press against her flesh.

She worked up the courage to speak. "You don't want to kill me, Roy," she said. "Zeke Stuart reminded you of your stepbrother, and that's why you wanted to kill him. But you don't really want to kill me."

Roy laughed, a high-pitched squeal. "You're trying to use psychology on me, I can tell. Do you know how I can tell?"

He whirled Grayson around. She faced him, looking into his eyes. She saw the look of an insane, rabid animal. In that instant she knew that there was not the slightest possibility of reasoning with him. He was completely mad.

"I talked to plenty of psychologists when they put me in that place they called a hospital, where they kept me locked in that awful little room. They didn't fool me, though. I fooled *them*." Roy drew his lips back from his teeth in a lizardlike imitation of a smile. "I invented ol' Slow-wits Degan. They thought Degan was a peachy guy, so they let me go."

Roy threw back his head and cackled . . . and cackled . . . and cackled. For a moment, Grayson thought he wasn't ever going to stop. Perhaps he *couldn't* stop. That's when she saw the length of two-by-four lying on the stairs.

As if her arm was not connected to her body, she saw her arm reach out, and saw her hand close around the two-by-four. Then her arm brought it swinging around, connecting with the man's head with a resounding *thwack!*

Grayson thought she had cracked his skull. She watched as he slipped to his knees and slid down the stairs to the landing below.

He was up in an instant, shaking his head vigorously from side to side. He climbed to his feet and looked up at Grayson with crazed eyes. He let out a howl of rage and clambered up the stairs toward her.

Holding the two-by-four tightly, Grayson took another wild swing. This time the wood connected with Roy's shoulder. She heard him grunt as it struck.

Grayson dropped the two-by-four and turned to run. Roy grabbed her ankle and held it in a viselike grip. Holding onto the banister, Grayson kicked out with her other foot. And connected with bone. She pulled her foot free and got moving. There was nowhere to go but up.

Roy was fast in pursuit. She heard him clunking along behind her. The sound of his heavy breathing filled the air.

Soon Grayson was pushing open the door

that led to the roof. She stepped out onto the asphalt surface and saw the stars.

It was a clear night, but the air was hot and thick. Still, it was cooler than the suffocating heat inside the warehouse. Grayson drew in great gulps of air.

Grayson began to run. She knew that she soon would reach the edge of the roof and there would be nowhere to go — yet she kept on running. There was nowhere to hide, and she didn't see anything on the flat expanse of roof that she could use to hit the man. She knew she didn't stand a chance against him with her bare hands.

The moment of truth was coming all too soon. The edge was barely ten feet away.

"Slow down, you'll spoil all the fun," Roy called out behind her.

From the sound of his voice, Grayson could tell that he was several feet away. Now that he was sure that victory was his, he had stopped running. She whirled around.

"Just back up one step at a time," Roy called. "That's the easiest thing to do. You won't even see the edge when you step off." He clapped his hands together. "Pretty soon, one, two, three, it's over, and I can go on about my business. Come on, Grayson. You know there's no way out."

I'll never do what he says, Grayson said to herself. I'll never just back away until I fall. I'll fight him every last minute, *no matter how hopeless it is*.

It was the sheer hopelessness of the situation that made Grayson take the chance that she did. She started running again, not toward the edge ten feet behind her, nor toward Roy. She knew she'd never get past him. This time she ran to the left in front of Roy, to the other side of the building.

At first Roy stood still. He was caught off guard, just as Grayson had prayed he would be.

"No!" he screamed in rage as he understood her plan. "You can't make it, you can't make it!"

They were the last words Grayson heard before she jumped.

Chapter 24

Please, please, please, Grayson prayed as she leaped into the air. She would either clear the chasm that separated the warehouse from the building that stood next to it, or die.

She looked longingly at the rooftop in front of her. It got closer and closer. *I'm going to make it, I'm going to make it, I'm going to make it, the thought spun around in circles inside her brain.*

But it looked as if her wish wasn't going to come true. Suddenly she wasn't flying through the air anymore. She was starting to drop down.

Please, Grayson prayed once more. She stretched out her arms, reaching, reaching. She squeezed her eyes shut tightly.

All the wind was knocked out of her as her body slammed against the building. Her eyes opened wide as she clawed her nails into the asphalt surface of the roof, fighting to hold on. But she slid backward, her fingers burning.

Just as Grayson was sure she would fall, her hands struck the lip at the edge of the roof. She gripped it hard and held on desperately.

"You've only got a couple minutes more," Roy called out to her. He laughed. "Would you like to say a few last words?"

Feeling as if her muscles would snap, Grayson gritted her teeth and pulled. She didn't budge. With every last ounce of strength, Grayson pulled again. Somehow she managed to pull herself up high enough to swing a leg over the edge of the building. Then, slowly, she made it the rest of the way.

Grayson knew she would never again feel as thankful as she did when her body collapsed on the asphalt roof. She stared up at the sky, tears streaming down her face.

"No!" She heard Roy cry out in rage. She rolled on her side and looked across at him. He was pacing back and forth like a caged animal. His face was so red, it looked as if his head might explode.

If I could jump across that space, he could make it easily, thought Grayson. Why isn't he moving?

Then it dawned on her. Roy was much more afraid of falling than she was.

"You're not going to get away!" Roy screamed. "I'll find a way to get to you. If not today, then tomorrow or the next day or the next. No psychic visions will help you, either. There isn't anything in the world that can keep you safe from me." Roy clenched his fists. "I won't be stopped! I *can't* be stopped!"

Grayson watched him. The horror of what had just happened swept over her in a wave. Feeling crashed back into her body at the same time. She felt as if she were one huge, single bruise from head to toe. Her entire body began to tremble. She wanted to run downstairs and out of the building, but she couldn't take a single step. It felt as if her legs were carved out of jelly.

Almost directly overhead, the Brooklyn Bridge rose into the sky. There you are, she thought. You were part of *my own murder* all along. She couldn't take her eyes off it.

Grayson stared at the bridge for a long time before she realized that Roy had stopped talking. When she looked at him, she was surprised to see that the color had drained from his face. His posture had changed, and he was clenching and unclenching his fists.

A bewildered look crept over the man's face. When he spoke, his voice didn't sound at all like Roy's. "What in the world is going on? What am I doing up here?" he shouted, wringing his hands. "Oh, my. Oh, my." He stared out over the edge of the building and stood still.

Grayson didn't know how long she sat watching the man. It could have been five minutes or five hours. He never moved. She thought she would never be able to move again, either.

She was wondering when the sun would come up when she saw something that made her eyes widen with surprise. Detective Soames was walking on the roof toward Degan.

Behind the detective were several police officers. Detective Soames walked over to where Degan was still standing and peering over the edge of the building.

"I don't know how I got here!" Degan screamed.

Grayson saw the detective motion the police officers to stay away.

"I don't think you want to know what happened here yet, Degan," Detective Soames said quietly. "It might upset you too much. We'll explain it all later. Just go with these men."

"The police?" Degan said, confused.

Detective Soames nodded. "That's right. You'll be safe with them."

Degan looked even more bewildered. "Okay," he said finally. He stood quietly as the police put handcuffs on him and led him away.

Grayson felt as if she'd been holding her breath for hours. She exhaled, and then took several deep breaths.

"Are you all right?" Detective Soames called.

"Yes!" Grayson managed to shout after a moment.

"Then hold on. I'm coming over to get you." For a moment, Grayson thought Detective Soames was going to leap right across to the building, but he didn't. He took the stairs. But he was by her side in a matter of seconds, it seemed.

"I'm so glad to see you!" Grayson exclaimed as the detective came toward her. "I don't think I could have got myself off this building for at least a couple of days."

Detective Soames smiled. "You'd stay here for a couple of days? Come on, Grayson, it's a nice place to *visit* . . ."

Grayson was surprised that she could laugh.

"Great!" said Detective Soames. "If you can laugh, you'll be fine."

"I *know* I'll be fine," Grayson said. "But how did you know where to find me?"

Detective Soames looked away for a moment, then looked back at Grayson. "Aileen told me," he said.

Chapter 25

Morning was just beginning to break across the sky. Already the air was muggy. Grayson stood beside Detective Soames and watched the lights of the police cruiser carrying William Roy Degan disappear as it turned at the end of the street. He's really gone, she said to herself, feeling a wave of relief.

An officer handed Grayson and the detective cups of coffee. Grayson wrapped her hands around the paper cup and watched the steam from the hot liquid float into the air. She turned to the detective. "You said you thought Aileen told you where to find me. Why?"

The detective nodded slowly. "That's what I think. It was strange. I know I was knocked out cold the moment Degan hit me with the hammer. But when I woke up, my head didn't hurt at all. I was wide awake and completely alert." The detective paused for a moment and looked as if he was searching for the best way to express his thoughts.

"I got right up and went straight to my car. Then I just started to drive. At that point I wasn't thinking, *where would this guy go?* the way I normally would have been. In fact, I wasn't thinking at all, I was just *doing.* I'd come to a corner, and it was as if something was guiding me, telling me to turn or go straight. I know it was Aileen." There wasn't the slightest trace of doubt in his voice.

"Aileen is the only one who could have known where you were," he went on. "In fact, I was so sure Aileen was showing me the way that I called for backup even before I saw you standing on the roof."

He looked down. "I'm glad it wasn't your sister, or your boyfriend," he said after a moment. "It turns out the construction crew manager wasn't supposed to hire nonunion labor. He never put Jared Moore's name on the list of employees."

The detective swallowed some coffee. "You know, I was starting to believe he was the one we were looking for. When I stopped by his house, one of the neighbors told me he'd packed up the car and left all of a sudden."

"Why didn't you tell me you suspected Jared

when you came to my apartment?"

"I didn't want to scare you."

Grayson stared into her coffee cup. "For a minute there, I thought it was *you.*"

"*Me?*" Detective Soames looked astonished. "Why?"

"Because you picked the lock to get into the apartment instead of knocking, and because of the weird glittering look I saw in your eyes."

"Oh, no," the detective groaned. He slapped his forehead with his palm. "Grayson, I knocked and knocked. When you didn't answer, I was afraid something had happened to you." He tugged at his earlobe. "As for that 'weird glittering look,' people have told me about it before. I think it happens when I think I'm close to catching a criminal."

Grayson took a sip of coffee. "You really knocked and knocked?"

"Yes. Really."

She shook her head. "I must have been off in another world." She took another sip of coffee. "It's so unbelievable to think that the killer was right in my building the whole time. It just seems so . . . fantastic."

The detective shrugged. "Criminals live someplace, just like everyone else does," he said with a half-smile. "It surprises people when they find the criminal lived next door, or across the street. Maybe they think they should live in special dorms."

"I suppose you're right." Grayson gave a little shudder. "It's still creepy."

"I know. Well, it looks like there's going to be a job opening in your building. You're going to need a new super." He laughed.

Grayson gave him a look of mingled surprise and disapproval. "I don't see how you can joke after what's just happened," she said.

"I guess it goes with the territory," Soames said after a moment. "If I let everything I saw on the job get to me, I couldn't do the job. It would bother me so much, I'd probably go crazy."

He smiled at Grayson. "So you see, I'm not such a tough guy. A little joke here and there helps me keep the bad stuff at a distance." He looked thoughtful. "You know, your psychic ability could be a big help to the police department. What would you say to working on some more cases?"

Grayson accidentally spilled a little of her coffee. "That's a tough one, Frank," she said. "In a way, I feel that I have to say yes. I think I should do all I can to help out. But . . ." She let her voice trail off.

"But what? You just said yourself that you

have an obligation to use your ability. How can you hesitate?"

Grayson set the paper cup of coffee down on the sidewalk. She crossed her arms. "You can understand, can't you? I'm not sure I want to be so close to crime and criminals all the time. I don't know if I can take having a life like that. Do you understand what I mean?"

"I suppose I understand. But when you get over this and calm down, I wish you'd think about it some more. You know how to reach me."

Grayson nodded. "I'll think about it after a while. Right now, I just want to go home. After that I want to try having a normal, ordinary life for a while. I want to think about boyfriends and girlfriends and having fun."

"Come on, I'll give you a ride."

"Thanks." Grayson followed the detective to his car. She settled back in the seat as he started the engine. The sun blazed in the sky. It's going to be another hot one, she thought.

Then she fell asleep.

Chapter 26

The radio news bulletin sent panic racing through Grayson's veins.

"Authorities at the facility for the criminally insane that houses killer William Roy Degan said that he escaped early this morning. It is thought that he left hidden in the back of a delivery truck.

"Two workers at a convenience store in Brooklyn, New York, reported seeing a man that fit Roy's description only a few hours ago. Police think he may be headed for his former place of residence in the Park Slope section.

"The most baffling feature of the case is the fact that Degan remains in custody. When told about Roy's escape, he appeared dazed and confused. He refused to comment."

Grayson sat up in bed, wide awake, her heart pounding. It was a nightmare, she told herself.

Besides, what happened in the dream was impossible. It just couldn't happen.

But in a way, she thought as she drifted back to sleep, it *did* happen. Degan was imprisoned, but Roy escaped every night . . . into her dreams.

Chapter 27

"Grayson! It's really great to see you again," Jared called as he walked across Mina's backyard.

Grayson watched him thread his way through the crowd of guests. She remembered how they had laughed and danced together at Mina's last barbecue. So much had happened since then.

Soon Jared was beside her. "I would have called you, but I just got back from a trip a couple of hours ago," he said. "I heard about what happened. You were very brave. It must have been terrifying."

"It was." Grayson nodded. "I had nightmares about it, but I haven't had them for the past couple of nights." She hadn't realized how much she missed Jared until now. "I haven't seen you for almost three weeks. Tell me about your trip."

"It wasn't for pleasure. I took my brother to stay with our aunt in Pennsylvania. He's going to be there at least until the end of the summer. He may even go to school there in the fall."

"Does it take a load off your mind?"

"Yeah. The best part of it is that he wanted to go. He thought it would help him stay away from that rough crowd he was hanging out with, and turn his life around."

Mina walked over. "How're you doing, guys? Did you just get here, Jared?"

"Uh-huh," Jared said, looking into Grayson's eyes.

"Uh-oh. I can see that I'd better leave you two alone," Mina said. "I think I'll go fire up the barbecue. If I hang around here, I probably won't get a word in edgewise, anyway."

"Imagine Mina not getting a word in edgewise," Jared laughed.

"She's terrific," said Grayson. "She was my first friend here in Brooklyn." She watched Mina walk away.

"You know," she said thoughtfully, "I was afraid of meeting new people at first. I was afraid all they'd want to talk about was my operation, and what it was like to be blind, as if I was some sort of interesting specimen."

"Well, I think you're interesting, but that's

not why," Jared said. "Now that things have calmed down for both of us, I'd like us to go out again. What do you say? How about Friday night?"

Grayson smiled. "I say it's a date."

Jared crossed his arms. "I've never gone out with a psychic before."

Grayson put her hand on his shoulder. "If you're worried about my reading your mind, forget it. As a matter of fact, I haven't had a single psychic vision since the case closed. My psychic powers have vanished. *Pouf!*" She snapped her fingers.

"You must be sorry."

Grayson shook her head. "Nope. Not a bit." She moved closer to Jared. "I'm actually relieved. How about you? Are you relieved I'm not psychic anymore?"

Jared didn't say anything. He kissed her instead.

NIGHTMARE HALL

where college is a scream!

THRILLERS

D.E. Athkins
- ❑ MC45246-0 Mirror, Mirror — $3.25
- ❑ MC45349-1 The Ripper — $3.25

A. Bates
- ❑ MC45829-9 The Dead Game — $3.25
- ❑ MC43291-5 Final Exam — $3.25
- ❑ MC44582-0 Mother's Helper — $3.25
- ❑ MC44238-4 Party Line — $3.25

Caroline B. Cooney
- ❑ MC44316-X The Cheerleader — $3.25
- ❑ MC41641-3 The Fire — $3.25
- ❑ MC43806-9 The Fog — $3.25
- ❑ MC45681-4 Freeze Tag — $3.25
- ❑ MC45402-1 The Perfume — $3.25
- ❑ MC44884-6 The Return of the Vampire — $2.95
- ❑ MC41640-5 The Snow — $3.99
- ❑ MC45680-6 The Stranger — $3.50
- ❑ MC45682-2 The Vampire's Promise — $3.50

Richie Tankersley Cusick
- ❑ MC43115-3 April Fools — $3.25
- ❑ MC43203-6 The Lifeguard — $3.25
- ❑ MC43114-5 Teacher's Pet — $3.25
- ❑ MC44235-X Trick or Treat — $3.50

Carol Ellis
- ❑ MC46411-6 Camp Fear — $3.25
- ❑ MC44768-8 My Secret Admirer — $3.25
- ❑ MC47101-5 Silent Witness — $3.25
- ❑ MC46044-7 The Stepdaughter — $3.25
- ❑ MC44916-8 The Window — $3.25

Lael Littke
- ❑ MC44237-6 Prom Dress — $3.50

Jane McFann
- ❑ MC46690-9 Be Mine — $3.25

Christopher Pike
- ❑ MC43014-9 Slumber Party — $3.50
- ❑ MC44256-2 Weekend — $3.50

Edited by T. Pines
- ❑ MC45256-8 Thirteen — $3.99

Sinclair Smith
- ❑ MC45063-8 The Waitress — $3.50

Barbara Steiner
- ❑ MC46425-6 The Phantom — $3.50

Robert Westall
- ❑ MC41693-6 Ghost Abbey — $3.25
- ❑ MC43761-5 The Promise — $3.25
- ❑ MC45176-6 Yaxley's Cat — $3.25

Available wherever you buy books, or use this order form.

Scholastic Inc., P.O. Box 7502, 2931 East McCarty Street, Jefferson City, MO 65102

Please send me the books I have checked above. I am enclosing $_____ (please add $2.00 to cover shipping and handling). Send check or money order — no cash or C.O.D.s please.

Name_____ Age _____

Address_____

City_____ State/Zip_____

Please allow four to six weeks for delivery. Offer good in the U.S. only. Sorry, mail orders are not available to residents of Canada. Prices subject to change.   T295

THRILLERS

Nobody Scares 'Em Like
R.L. Stine

Some girls would *kill* to go to the prom!

Prom DATE

BY DIANE HOH

Stephanie, Liza, Kiki, and Beth are
the most popular girls in school.
When Prom Night comes, they're always
there with the *cutest* guys.
But this year is going to be different.
Someone doesn't want them at the prom.
Someone wants them dead.

Coming to a bookstore near you.

HORT 1095